Amy Cheng likes to travel to different places to take photos, draw, and get ideas for her stories. For those places, she would think about characters and unusual plots different from the real world like the story *The Adventures of the Unknown Worlds* and another book *My Incredible Adventures*.

For my family and friends

Amy Cheng

THE ADVENTURES OF THE UNKNOWN WORLDS

AUSTIN MACAULEY PUBLISHERS™

LONDON • CAMBRIDGE • NEW YORK • SHARJAH

Copyright © Amy Cheng 2022

All rights reserved. No part of this publication may be reproduced, distributed, or transmitted in any form or by any means, including photocopying, recording, or other electronic or mechanical methods, without the prior written permission of the publisher, except in the case of brief quotations embodied in critical reviews and certain other noncommercial uses permitted by copyright law. For permission requests, write to the publisher.

Any person who commits any unauthorized act in relation to this publication may be liable to criminal prosecution and civil claims for damages.

This is a work of fiction. Names, characters, businesses, places, events, locales, and incidents are either the products of the author's imagination or used in a fictitious manner. Any resemblance to actual persons, living or dead, or actual events is purely coincidental.

Ordering Information
Quantity sales: Special discounts are available on quantity purchases by corporations, associations, and others. For details, contact the publisher at the address below.

Publisher's Cataloging-in-Publication data
Cheng, Amy
The Adventures of the Unknown Worlds

ISBN 9781645750819 (Paperback)
ISBN 9781645750802 (Hardback)
ISBN 9781645750826 (ePub e-book)

Library of Congress Control Number: 2021911748

www.austinmacauley.com/us

First Published 2022
Austin Macauley Publishers LLC
40 Wall Street, 33rd Floor, Suite 3302
New York, NY 10005
USA

mail-usa@austinmacauley.com
+1 (646) 5125767

Thanks to everyone in the Austin Macauley team who took the time to work on my book and make my dream come true.

Part I

Chapter 1

The bell was ringing, and the hallway was crowded with students running to their classrooms. Catherine Fong didn't know where to go on her first day as a high-school freshman. She saw a girl passing by, so she asked her where the class was and what time it was. Once she knew where to go, she ran to that room. That class was just a homeroom where Catherine met her first classmate, Fanny. The teacher took attendance, and then all the students were dismissed, and they went to their other classes.

During math class, she met the girl who had helped her earlier. Her name was Lillian. They soon became friends because they had most classes together, including lunch. Lillian introduced Catherine to another friend, Sophia, who had the same lunch period as them. Sophia told them a legend:

A long time ago, there was a magical old pink Sakura (cherry blossom) tree that turned animals into humans. However, the tree had to look for an animal that was kind-hearted enough to take care of the tree. For a long time, no animal really loved or took care of the tree; they all treated it roughly, hitting it and throwing junk at it.

After hearing the legend, Catherine told them it was true. They asked her why she thought that, but she couldn't tell them. She believed the story because she remembered the boy she had met half a year ago.

***

Six months ago, Catherine had met Alan, who was a panda.

He was walking around in a peaceful area surrounded by waterfalls, trees, mountains, flowers, and rocks. As he was passing by the sakura tree, he stopped and turned back. He stood in front of the tree and said, "Wow, what a nice tree! You're so lonely. Are you alone?"

Suddenly rain began pouring down. The panda used a gigantic leaf to cover all the petals and hug the tree trunk, but the wind came and blew them off. All of a sudden, the panda felt dizzy and collapsed to the ground, unconscious.

The next day, the tree disappeared, and the panda woke up. Unbeknown to him, he'd undergone a magic spell, and his appearance changed to that of a human being. The first thing he noticed was the missing tree. He looked everywhere; he searched for ten days without food or water, but he couldn't find it. Eventually, he collapsed.

A day later, Catherine saw him lying on the ground. She shook him, but he wasn't moving, so she yelled for help. Of course, no one came, so she dragged him into the shade by his shirt. After a while, he woke up. She took her water bottle out of her schoolbag and told him to drink some water from it. She noticed that he was actually a handsome young boy around her age. Suddenly, her heart was pounding very quickly. She thought something was wrong with her heart.

He said, "Thanks for saving me. No one has treated me so nicely before. Are you terrified of my appearance?"

Catherine laughed and said, "You're welcome. You're funny. Of course, I'm not afraid of you. You're a handsome young boy. By the way, my name is Catherine. What's your name?"

The panda was surprised and said, "I have no name. I'm just a panda."

"What are you talking about? You're a panda and have no name? No, you're a handsome boy. I have a mirror here. Take a look at yourself."

The panda looked at the mirror and was shocked by his appearance. It was the first time he noticed the change in his body.

"What happened to my face and body? When did I turn into a human? Before I passed out, I protected the sakura tree from the heavy rain. That was it."

"I don't know what happened to you. In the meantime, you can't stay out here in the elements. Do you want to stay at my brother, Raymond's house?"

"I don't want to bother your brother. I'm glad you're not fearful of me now that you know I'm not a human."

"No! You're not a bother. You're not scary at all. Just stay with my brother. He is a nice person who likes to assist others. I think you're a kind being. There are many others who wouldn't have treated the tree as nicely as you did. I am sure you and my brother will become friends soon."

"Thanks for taking me in. I cared for that sakura tree because I really love all different kinds of trees, especially sakura trees. I felt that tree was special. I have never seen a tree like that."

"You're such a warm panda. When I saw you at the beginning, I just had a feeling that I should take care of you. We should probably give you a name so I can introduce you to my brother, though."

"Sure, what is my name going to be?"

"Hmmm…how about Alan Pan?"

"OK, MY NAME IS ALAN FROM NOW ON."

Alan and Catherine left the lovely garden, which unbeknown to them was a secret and magical area. Catherine brought Alan to her brother's home on Ping On Street in the city of New York. Alan was amazed by his surroundings. Even though he was a human, he still moved like a panda, which drew some strange expressions from the people he passed.

They both entered the apartment and walked up to Raymond's home. Luckily, Raymond happened to be there. He was astonished to see Catherine entering his house with a guy.

"Let me introduce my friend to you. His name is Alan, and he has no place to sleep. Do you mind taking him in as your roommate since you are alone here?" said Catherine.

"Hi, Alan. I'm Raymond. Please let me talk to my sister privately in the other room," said Raymond. He was trying to figure out whether or not Alan was Catherine's boyfriend. Alan waited outside in the living room.

"Catherine, tell me what is happening here. Is he your boyfriend? Does he have a place to live? Where's his family?" asked Raymond.

"Actually, I don't know him, but I know he is a kind person." Catherine told Raymond all the details of what had happened at the garden. Raymond was shocked and a little skeptical but decided to help Alan. If nothing else, it would enable him to keep a closer eye on this stranger's relationship with his sister.

"Oh, one more thing: we will have to train him to be a human living in the human world." Raymond agreed, and they went out of the room.

"My brother decided to let you stay here."

Alan faced Raymond. "Really? Thanks a lot, Raymond." Raymond just smiled and showed him around the house.

Catherine checked the time and rushed to put on her jacket and shoes. "I have to go home to cook for Mom now. I will visit you guys again tomorrow."

The next day, Catherine and Raymond started to teach Alan how to act like a human. Alan was excited to start the training. They taught him as many daily activities as they could—things like walking properly, taking a bath, changing clothes, observing table manners, writing, counting money, using transportation, cleaning the house, cooking, and grocery shopping. Alan was a fast learner. After about a month, he was presentable to others.

***

Sophia and Lillian called Catherine, snapping her out of her reverie. Lunch period had ended, and they attended the next class. In science class, Catherine got a pass to use the restroom. While she was gone, a new male student arrived late. He introduced himself to the teacher and classmates as Alan.

When Catherine returned to the classroom, she noticed the new student at the back. She felt a strange pull to this boy who was listening to his music player and wearing a cross-body bag. He turned around, and Catherine was astounded to see her old panda friend. It had been two months since he'd disappeared.

As soon as the class ended, Catherine ran to Alan. "Where have you been these two months? My brother and I were searching for you all over the place."

Alan looked confused. "Sorry, I don't know you. I think you've got the wrong person."

"You don't remember me? I'm Catherine. I gave you the name of Alan." It seemed like Catherine was a total stranger to Alan. Alan left the classroom to go to his next class.

Catherine believed he would remember her someday. There was no use asking him questions about his past. She didn't even have a photo with him. Therefore, she decided to start from the beginning. The first step was becoming his friend again. However, it was hard to approach him as a stranger, even as a classmate, so they didn't talk for a week.

After one week of school, Catherine was already used to the high-school life and enjoying her time with friends, but she wasn't focusing on her studies. Her art teacher assigned Catherine to the back row in a seat next to Alan and asked them to share a textbook. Catherine was surprised and ecstatic; her heart was pounding very fast. She thought she would never get close to him. She heard the teacher call him Alan and felt elated that he still remembered the name she'd given him, even if he had forgotten about other things.

They didn't start a conversation during the first class. It started in the second class when Alan asked Catherine about the homework. After that, they talked nonstop. They would also joke most of the time. Lillian and other classmates thought they were dating each other. Very often, their art teacher had to ask them to stop talking in class; they even lost a few points on their grades because of their chatting. Still, Catherine scored high in art since she was really good at drawing and it was an area that she liked the most. Plus, she was able to talk to Alan. The class always felt very short compared with other classes even though all the periods were of the same length of time.

In one of the art classes, Catherine's and Alan's eyes met for what seemed like an eternity. Then their hands accidentally touched while using the same handout. To shift the attention, Catherine started to have a real conversation with Alan about his current life and his lost memories. As far as she knew, she and Raymond were the only humans he'd known. Catherine asked, "Who are you living with now?"

"I am living with my guardian in a small apartment. I don't remember if he is my family member or not, but he treats me like his son. He even helped me to apply to this school," he answered.

What a coincidence, Catherine thought, *that the guardian had happened to help him to apply at her school.* She wanted to ask more questions, but the bell rang to signal the end of the period.

They rarely communicated in other classes because they had their own friends there, but sometimes her eyes would follow Alan. Once in a while, Alan would put candies on her desk when she was resting her head there. Then he would wake her up by knocking on her desk. He would also walk to Catherine's table at the library to ask her about schoolwork while their friends were there. Sometimes during lunchtime, Alan and his best friend sat at Catherine's table to talk to Catherine and her friends. Most of the time, Alan sat with his boys' group, and Catherine sat with her girls' group. She was glad Alan was open to others.

Besides talking in art class, Catherine and Alan began to chat online at a specific time after school. Catherine looked forward to chatting with him. They also liked to borrow items from each other and listened to each other's favorite songs. Catherine enjoyed her current relationship with Alan by taking things at a slow pace. Their calm relationship as classmates and friends continued until a popular girl got transferred to the school.

Chapter 2

Second semester changed things. Instead of having three classes of art per week, Catherine and Alan had only two art classes each week. Also, a popular transfer student named Tina sat in front of Catherine in science class. She was smart, tall, pretty, and outgoing. Tina talked a lot with both boys and girls, exuding a confidence Catherine didn't have.

Catherine wanted to confess her feelings to Alan, but she was shy and felt it was more traditional for him to come to her. In addition, she was afraid of being rejected by him. She didn't have much confidence in herself and decided to give up on him. *He was too tall for her anyway,* she thought. And he got along so easily with Tina. That would be a better match. Never mind that Alan and Tina didn't talk much and that Tina could have her pick of the boys at school.

In the next art class, Catherine tried to ignore Alan even though he was trying to talk to her. "You are quiet today, what happened?" asked Alan.

"Nothing," said Catherine.

"You seem to be in a bad mood."

"I already said nothing's wrong. Please leave me alone." Then, they kept silent for the rest of the class. Lillian was astounded that they didn't talk to each other.

Catherine even started blowing off their online chat. In the following few weeks, Alan developed a bad mood, even losing his temper toward his friends. Catherine felt uneasy and miserable when she ignored him.

The one person who loved this situation was Tina. She asked Alan's best friend, Joseph, what had happened to Alan, and Joseph said, "He broke up with Catherine." Then Tina faced Catherine and asked her about her relationship with Alan, but Catherine just ignored Tina's question. Tina smiled and was now confident that she could snag Alan since she had better qualities than Catherine.

While Catherine and Alan were in a bad relationship, a boy named Jay joined Catherine's math class. His seat was next to hers, and Catherine and Jay soon became friends. They lived close to each other, so they walked home from school together every day. They even did their math homework together during lunch time. Alan saw them but didn't say anything. Catherine noticed Alan looking at her direction.

Jay and Alan attended the same global history class. One day, Alan faced Jay and asked, "Do you love Catherine?"

Jay was shocked. "Hmmm…why are you asking that question? What's your relationship with her?"

"We are just friends. Why are you asking me questions? I questioned you first," Alan countered aggressively.

His tone put Jay on the defensive. "Yes, I have some feelings for her. And I know you like her, but you had your chance; I won't lose to you."

Alan jumped from his chair and cocked his arm to take a swing. Jay just pushed Alan back to stop him. The teacher,

Mr. Brown, ran over to stop them. Alan retreated, saying, "You stay away from Catherine." Mr. Brown warned them to see him after class.

Lillian, who was also in that class, told Catherine about what had happened. Catherine was stunned and went to check on Jay during lunch time. She asked, "Are you OK?"

"I'm fine," said Jay.

"Alan is wrong. He misunderstands that you like me."

"No, he doesn't. I do have feelings for you."

"He has no right to try to hit you. Wait...you have feelings for me?"

"Yes, since the first time I met you."

"Jay, I'm sorry. I—I cannot return that love. You're a good friend, but that's all I see you as."

"No, you don't have to apologize. I know you don't like me like that. I always see you looking at Alan. That's why I didn't say anything until Alan questioned me how I felt about you. I was planning to hide that from you. Anyway, I will still protect you and be your friend. Do you really like Alan that much?"

"Thanks for your support. Yes, I liked him before school started. Actually, things are complicated between us."

"Well, whenever you need to talk to someone, let me know. I will be there for you anytime and anywhere."

Catherine left, and Jay just sat inside the classroom daydreaming until class was over.

Catherine stayed mad at Alan for attacking Jay. One day, Alan came over to look for her at the library while she was doing homework with Lillian. He said, "Can I talk to you alone for a few minutes?" Catherine didn't say anything, and Lillian went to another table far away.

"What do you want to talk about? I have nothing to say to you," said Catherine, looking at her textbook.

Alan snatched the textbook away. "Why won't you even look at me? Is this about the thing with Jay? I took a swing at him because I am so angry and confused. We were fine before, and then suddenly you two were inseparable. Do you love him?"

"You shouldn't have hit him," she said flatly. "He did nothing wrong. He and I are just friends, just like you and I who are just friends, nothing more and nothing less. I am not mad at you. That's it." Alan left.

Catherine was crying, and Lillian came over to sit beside her. She said, "What's wrong with you? You two are made for each other. When you guys are in art class, I feel you are in your own world. I heard Alan telling Joseph that he loves you."

Catherine said, "It's probably another Catherine."

"Please, there aren't that many Catherines in this school, plus you are the closest to him. Think about this: Maybe the reason Alan wanted to fight Jay is that he was fearful you were in love with Jay or that Jay would steal you away from him."

"Don't be silly. What about our huge height difference? Tina is a much better match for him—tall, not to mention intelligent and beautiful."

"Tina? I think you are cuter than she is. You always have cute smile. I like that side of you. I don't think Tina and Alan are that close. They don't talk to each other like you and Alan did. You guys talk nonstop."

"It's not just the height difference. I actually met Alan before I came to this school."

"What? Really? Tell me the whole story."

"He was actually a panda that turned into human by the magic tree that he took care of. Since he had nowhere to go, I put him at my brother's home, but then he went missing for two months and didn't recognize me when he came here. I believe he has amnesia. I want to know what happened in those two months. Sure, he says he's in love with me now, but what about then? If he remembers his past, how can he explain leaving?"

"Oh, my god, this sounds like the legend that Sophia told us."

"Please don't tell anyone about this secret."

"My lips are sealed."

Lillian left the table to go to the restroom. Catherine was in her own world, thinking about when Alan was still living in her brother's home.

***

During Alan's training to be a human, Catherine taught him to walk, eat, write, speak, and behave properly. "You have to walk properly. Stand up straight!" said Catherine. She put a book on top of his head to work on his balance. Each time he dropped the book, he was not allowed to eat his favorite food which was bamboo, and Catherine would add an additional book on his head. He ended up having ten thin books on his head. As he improved, she would remove a book at a time.

He also trained to write neatly by copying words and definitions in the dictionary and engaged in conversations with her and Raymond to improve his language skill. Then she showed him videos on table manners and using chopsticks and cutlery to eat like a human. To work on his people skills, she showed him dramas and taught him the correct way to interact with others.

Day by day, Catherine developed a deep affection for Alan. Whenever she saw him, her heart started racing, and her face blushed like a tomato, to the point where Alan thought she was wearing makeup. She was afraid to tell him, however; would he even know what that meant? On the other hand, she didn't want to live to regret keeping quiet. One night, she told him how she felt. She said, "You don't have to answer me now. How about we meet at the Japanese restaurant across from here tomorrow at 1:00 p.m.? You can let me know the answer then."

"OK," said Alan.

The next day, Catherine waited at the restaurant for three hours, and he didn't come. She went home and saw a note. It said, "Catherine, I can't accept your confession. We're from different worlds. I don't want you to see my current condition. Thanks for taking care of me. I will remember you forever. Take care!" She started to cry and ran out of the house. She looked all over the neighborhood, but he was nowhere to be found.

***

Lillian tapped on Catherine's shoulder. The bell rang, and they went to art class together. Catherine took out the note that Alan had left those months ago. She has carried the note with her since Alan showed up at the school. Alan saw she was holding the paper sadly. He was wondering who wrote it to her. He walked quietly behind her and read the note; he was shocked by what he was seeing. He said, "Who wrote that to you?"

"Why were you reading someone else's paper? That is so rude. I don't have to report it to you," said Catherine furiously.

"Is it Jay or another guy? I want to know."

"Why did you bring up Jay again? He has nothing to do with it. If you want to know, then try to remember yourself. You should know better than me."

"Why are you talking like I am the one who wrote you that note? I don't recall writing anything to you. I didn't even know you before I came to this school."

"Never mind. We will talk about this after you remember." The teacher came in, so Alan went back to his seat, confused. At that moment, Tina saw Alan and ducked into the classroom even though she wasn't supposed to be in that class. Tina tried to seduce him by showing her sexy dress.

"How do I look in this dress?" asked Tina.

"I'm not in the mood now. Leave!" said Alan angrily. Tina stormed off, glaring at Catherine. Catherine just ignored her and looked at her notebook.

After class, Catherine headed toward the library to read a book. On her way there, she saw Jay at the staircase. They went to the library together. There weren't many students inside the library. Jay returned his books while Catherine searched for a book. She was focused on her search for the book. What she didn't see was a tall and huge bookshelf full of books falling down.

Jay rushed over and pulled her to the side. The bookshelf hit his head, drawing blood. "Are you OK, Catherine?" asked Jay dizzily.

"I am fine. You are bleeding; don't talk too much. I will tell the teacher to call an ambulance," said Catherine. Jay then fainted, which terrified Catherine. She was so worried that she rode with him in the ambulance to the hospital.

At the hospital, she sat outside the room while the doctors tended to Jay. She prayed and promised to accept Jay's affections if he was OK. The doctor came out and told them that Jay was stable now but still need to have a head CT scan to make sure everything was all right. His family members nodded, and Jay was sent to a regular room.

Catherine walked into the room to see Jay, who was already awake. She walked over to his bed. "How are you feeling now?" Catherine asked worriedly.

"I am fine," said Jay.

"That's good. I am sorry."

"It's not your fault. It was an accident. I don't regret saving you. I would do the same thing again if it happened."

"No, don't say that. I don't want you to be sent to the hospital again because of me." They looked at each other silently, and his family left quietly.

"Listen, I've been thinking about what you said, and I think I was wrong. I think we can try to date each other."

"I don't want you to date me just because I saved you. I know you love Alan."

"It's not just that you saved me. It is true I still love Alan. It takes some time to forget about that love, but I want to try to move on."

"Are you sure? I don't want to force you."

"Yup, you didn't force me."

"Yeah!" He smiled and hugged her.

"Don't get too excited. You are still sick and need more rest."

"Yes, madam! I will listen to you." They laughed.

After a week, Jay's head CT result was normal, so he was discharged from the hospital. He didn't want to miss school, so he went the next day, holding hands with Catherine. Their classmates asked them when they'd gotten together. Jay felt embarrassed and admitted that it was while he was in the hospital.

Alan saw them together and lost it. He ran out to the hallway, climbed up to the top floor, and banged the wall with his fist until his hand was swollen and bleeding. Tina saw him and walked over to hug him. Alan shouted, "Get away from me."

Tina said, "Why? Why Catherine? What's so good about her? I am much better than her in almost everything."

"Love is not about comparing two people to see which one has better qualities. I have no feeling for you." Tina kissed him on his lips, but he pushed her away.

"Don't make me hate you. You have no chance even though she has a boyfriend now. I will hold out for her until I die."

"Why do you love her so much?"

"I am not sure, but maybe that's love. I loved her at first sight."

"I won't believe I lost to her. I won't give up on you."

"Why do you go that far for me?"

"I love you; that's the reason. More importantly, I don't want to lose to her. I have never lost to another girl, especially to a loser. Other guys, even ones with girlfriends, are all fighting for me."

"That's not love. You don't love me, and you don't know the meaning of love. You love yourself and the feeling of winning others. Love is when you want your loved one to be happy, even if that's not with you." Tina walked away, only to be stopped by a teacher, who sent her to the principal's office.

The principal, the guidance counselor, and Tina's parents were all in the office. Tina felt uneasy. Another student came into the room. The counselor asked, "You said you witnessed Tina pushing the bookshelf purposely to hurt Catherine, is that correct?"

The student said, "Yes, I saw her."

Tina's parents yelled at Tina and asked for forgiveness from counselor, and principal. The principal said, "This is a serious act, so Tina needs to be suspended from school." Soon, the whole school knew about what Tina did to Catherine. Tina didn't return to school after the suspension period. Rumor had it that she had transferred to another school.

One month before the end of the semester, Catherine told her friends that she was transferring to another school because her family was moving. She had already been accepted into one of the high schools close to her new home. She wished time would go by gradually so she could spend more time with her friends. She decided to talk to Alan before leaving the school. Alan was down but still wished her good luck at the new school. She smiled and said, "Thanks." Then, she left quietly. While walking to her class, Jay found Catherine, and asked her out for a date to the Sky Stars Adventure Land on that coming Sunday. She agreed to it.

On the day of their date, Jay met Catherine in front of her apartment. Jay held her hand when they were on the train to the Sky Stars Adventure Land. She was kind of quiet, so he tried to pick a topic to talk about it. "What do you want to do first?" he asked.

"Hmmm…it's up to you. I am not really into fast rides," said Catherine.

"OK, no scary rides. How about we try the bumper cars and teacups ride, shop around, eat, and ride the Ferris wheel?"

"That's a good idea. Thanks for being so understanding."

"You are my girlfriend, so I want you to have fun and be comfortable with me."

She smiled. "You are a gentle person."

They arrived at the Sky Stars Adventure Land. Jay's stomach was growling, so Catherine suggested they go eat first. They went to a cute café to eat. Eating seemed to improve Catherine's mood. Jay said, "It is good to see you smile. Please smile more! I want you to be happy every day." She beamed and nodded her head.

After eating, they went to the arcade area. Jay played the water-gun game, and he won a big stuffed animal for Catherine. She played another game where she was trying to throw balls into one of the jars. She managed to land one in the jar, so she got a goldfish, and she gave it to Jay as an exchange gift. Then, they went to drive the bumper cars and ride the teacups ride.

It was almost evening by the time they finished eating, riding, and playing games. Their last ride was the Ferris wheel. At the top, Jay leaned closer and tried to kiss her, but she pushed him away and looked out of the window.

"Are you thinking about Alan? You still can't forget about Alan," said Jay disappointedly.

"Sorry, please give me some time. I thought it may be easy to forget about him," said Catherine.

"You shouldn't have to force yourself. I really do want you to be happy every day. Ever since we've been together, I haven't seen a natural smile from you. I know you try very hard, but you don't have to pretend to smile when you are sad."

"You're such a good person, and I don't want to upset you."

"I know you like me, but you don't love me. Let's end here."

"Sorry."

"You don't have to apologize. Thanks for giving me a chance to be with you and make good memories. I still love you, but I will keep this love in my heart and to myself. I will still protect and watch over you. Please do me a favor."

"What is it?"

"Smile! Don't keep your love to yourself. I know you and Alan love each other. Go ahead and talk to him."

"I don't want you to just think about me. I also want you to be content. You have to smile, too. I hope you will find your love one someday. You don't have to protect me. You already did too much for me, and I didn't do anything for you."

"Love does not depend on how much you or I sacrifice for each other. Are we still friends?"

"Yup, you are my good friend forever."

They finished the Ferris wheel ride and took the train home. Jay walked Catherine to her apartment. He walked home feeling miserable and wasn't able to sleep that night.

The next day, Catherine saw Jay at school, and they greeted each other like nothing happened before. She went to her classes as usual. Alan went to Jay and asked him, "You guys seem to be different. Did anything happen?"

"Yup, we broke up yesterday."

"Why? I thought you were in love. You even threw yourself in the path of danger."

"Because she doesn't love me. She only likes me as a friend, nothing more and nothing less. We are still friends. I know she loves you, and you also love her. So seriously, one of you needs to take the first step; otherwise, you guys will remain like this forever."

"I know."

"You better do something. Please support and protect her. Make her smile!"

"I will! Why are you supporting me? You don't hate me?"

"I just want Catherine to be happy." They both smiled.

"Thanks. From now on, I will protect her." They shook hands.

Soon, it was the last day of the semester. Sophia was also going to another school, but Lillian, Alan, and everyone else would be back next semester. Even though their time together was winding down, Alan didn't get a chance to talk seriously with Catherine about their relationship. However, they were able to talk normally like before, so he wanted to take one step at a time.

Chapter 3

Catherine started her new semester at an unfamiliar school. Everything was new to her, and she missed the old school a lot. Without her good friends there, she devoted all her time to studying and doing her homework every day after school. Even in school, she always went to the school library to study or do her homework during lunch. Her academics improved a lot, from average student to honor-roll student. However, she spent less time on her hobbies, like origami, puzzles, and drawing.

During Christmas week, she was able to take a break to work on her old pastimes as well as contact her old friends. Catherine and Alan only talked for a few minutes on the phone, but after that call, they started online chatting and texting each other. She felt like they were back to the old days in school. They were always joking until one day Alan suddenly got serious and confessed his feelings to her. She thought he was joking, so she just changed the subject. He tried again though email, but she still thought it was a joke. He even took time to complete a one-thousand-piece puzzle and bought a big stuffed animal for her. He called her to come get the gift but didn't mention the lingering question about their relationship. In return, she made him a scarf and a jar with stars that she folded using origami paper strips.

After Christmas week, Catherine went back to school. She continued to be a top student focused on school, but each day, she looked forward to chat with Alan online. One day he revealed he had already dropped out of high school. She suggested him to go back to school or get a GED to go to college, but he didn't listen.

Alan called her when he was off from his part-time job. At first, she didn't know where he was working until she saw him working at a sushi restaurant she happened to be at with her friend. He immediately went in the kitchen to make her a salmon roll and a sashimi dish. Her friend was surprised the portion was so large. *It was so sweet of him,* she thought. That night, Catherine texted him and asked him out for a date. Alan was excited to meet her the next day. Catherine was nervous because she was scared he would disappear again like before.

The next day, as she was crossing the street to go meet him, a car sped through a red light and hit her badly. One of the bystanders called the ambulance, and she was taken to the emergency room. Alan waited for her for two hours before he got a call from her—well, from someone at the hospital telling him that Catherine was in the emergency room.

As if Catherine's injury weren't enough, a big block nearly fell on him as he made his way to the hospital. He was fine, but the near miss triggered his past memories. He remembered who he was, how he'd met Catherine, and why he'd disappeared.

***

After Catherine had declared her feelings to him during their training, she went back to her room leaving him in the living room. Then, he went back to Raymond's home.

He wasn't able to fall asleep that night. He was scared to be with her because they were from different worlds. He was a panda and she was a human; what kind of future could they have? He didn't even know how he'd turned into a human, let alone whether it was permanent.

Alan tossed and turned all night until he finally left the house and sat at the park. There was a man sitting next to him at the bench. He sighed and said to the man, "I have a girl that I love, but we are from two different worlds. I know she loves me, but I haven't answered her yet. We are meeting tomorrow to talk about it. What should I do?"

The man said, "I think you should accept her declaration. We don't know what will happen in the next moment. We may or may not be in this world any second. You should enjoy your time with her until the last minute. It doesn't matter how long our lifespan is; the importance is how we spend our time. Living a long life without happiness is meaningless. When my wife was alive, I only cared about working and making money. Now she's gone, and I regret that I didn't spend much time with her."

"Sorry to hear about your loss. You are right; I just concern that Catherine will be dejected someday when I leave her. Maybe it's better for her not to start the relationship with me at all."

"I understand your worry, but that doesn't change the fact that you have to enjoy every moment until the last."

"Yup, you're right. We should live in the moment without any regret. Thanks for listening to me." Alan left the park and went home to sleep.

He decided once and for all to return Catherine's affections. However, when he looked at the mirror, he saw his panda's ears popping out and his stomach turning bigger. He covered himself with a cap. Then he went to Catherine's home, left a note under the door, and took a taxi to the garden where they'd met. He was sitting on the ground where he found the magic sakura tree before. At that moment, he was totally turned back into a panda.

After six hours, Catherine arrived at the secret garden, too. As soon as Alan saw her, he quickly hid behind a normal tree. He didn't want her to see him as a panda. Catherine thought that was the first place they met. She shouted, "Where are you? I really miss you. I really don't mind how you look. I just want to be with you." He waited until she left the garden, and then he came out.

He was praying and begging that he would turn back into a human. He stayed for two days and one night, searching for the magic sakura tree. He didn't know that the tree was invisible. It was actually watching him search. Finally, noting how patient he was, the tree appeared in front of him. He was so glad to see the tree again, saying, "You finally appear. I have been looking all over the place for you. Why did I turn back into a panda? Is there a way to turn me back into a human?"

"You are originally a panda. There is a time limit for my magic to work on you," said the tree.

"I don't mind a time limit as long as you can turn me into a human again. I want to go see Catherine and tell her that I love her. She is waiting for me now."

"Actually, I want to help you, but my magic is not currently working because my master is punishing me for turning you into human. I have no magic for one year."

"I don't want you to get into trouble again for turning me into a human. I guess my fate with Catherine ends here."

"I can't use my magic, but there's a way for you to turn into a human. I buried a magic water bottle underground a thousand years ago. You have to find it because I forget where I put it."

"OK, I will look for it, but what is that for?"

"After finding the water bottle, you pour exactly five drops into the lake there. Remember, no less or more than five drops. Those five drops of water will open the other dimension for you. You have to go there to find a pill that has a sakura shape on it. There's only one pill like that from the dimension, so don't worry, you will recognize it when you see it. It's at a cave. You will see many sakura trees outside of the cave."

"Listen carefully. The pill is useful for turning you back into a human or saving the life of someone important to you. Remember to eat the whole pill. Eating half pill will also turn you back into a human, but only temporarily. I'm not sure of the time limit on that. However, you have the option to take half pill for yourself and give the other half to save your important one in the future. You should also know that taking the pill may have dangerous consequences. One last thing: You have to get the pill and come back to Earth in twenty-four hours. Otherwise you won't be able to return.

The gate will be closed in twenty-four hours in that dimension."

"OK, I got it. I am not afraid of consequences. I only care about seeing Catherine again." Alan searched the ground for half a month of days and nights. One night, he found the bottle near the orchid flower. He quickly went to the lake to pour in five drops of water. The lake water began turning clockwise at a rapid rate, and then Alan jumped into the hole, flowing through into another dimension.

The other dimension called Ever Sakura Dimension reminded Alan of the Edo period in Japan, which had many traditional wooden houses and stores with tiled roofs. Creatures used sliding doors and wooden furniture. Those creatures looked like half human on the top and half bear on the bottom. He also saw temples and shrines. As for entertainment, creatures enjoyed to watch stage plays at traditional theatres. It was a busy town full of creatures. He half expected to see ninja and samurai. He walked into different stores to ask creatures about the sakura cave, but no one had heard of it. He didn't give up and just continued to ask creatures. He walked into a tea store.

"Can you tell me where the cave surrounded by sakura trees is?" he asked the owner there.

The owner said, "Oh, the cave; I know where that is, but it's dangerous to go to that cave. You will encounter many hazards."

"I really need to go there. How long does it take to reach it?"

"Probably five hours walking from here." The owner then told him the direction to the cave, and he set off. After he left, the owner wondered whether he'd gave the right direction to the panda, seeing as he had no sense of direction.

Alan moved as fast as he could. He traveled a long distance but still didn't see the cave. He was concerned he'd be unable to go back to the gate on time. Then he saw an old lady carrying a heavy item. He stopped the old lady and aided her carry the item to her home even though it used up half an hour of his limited time. When they arrived at the old lady's home, she offered him a cup of sakura tea. When Alan saw the sakura flowers inside the cup, he asked, "Where did you get these sakura flowers from?"

The old lady said, "Sakura trees are popular here, so you can get it anywhere here."

"Is there a cave close to many sakura trees?"

The old lady took him outside. "Yes, you have to cross that mountain there," she said, pointing, "and then you will see the cave." Alan thanked her for the tea, and she thanked him for his help. Alan left the house and took off toward the mountain. Eventually, he saw the cave with many sakura trees outside. It was a pretty landscape. As Alan approached the cave to get the sakura pill, a fairy appeared.

"Hi, I'm the fairy here to look after the sakura pill. I have been here for ten generations. Before you can get the pill, you have to pass a test to see if you are the real owner of the pill. Here's the test: You have to eat one of the sakura trees. Most of them are poisonous, so I have to test your bravery. See if you can find the one sakura tree that has no poisoned petals. The rest are a mix of both poisonous and not poisonous. I want to see if you are the right person to have the pill," said the fairy.

Alan decided to take the risk. He looked around and chose the one in the middle on the left side. He ate all the sakura petals. He didn't feel anything at all. "Did I pass the test? I didn't die," said Alan.

"Yes, you passed the test. The pill is for you. You may go inside the cave to get the pill." She cleared the outside barrier and allowed him to enter the cave.

He went into a dark cave, and then he saw something bright shining all the way at the back. It was the pill, tucked inside a transparent box. He snatched the pill from the box and ran out of the cave, elated. "Thanks, fairy."

"You are welcome. I have finished my job here, so I am going now."

"Where are you going? Will I see you again?"

"I may or may not see you, but it was our fate to meet each other today." The fairy vanished.

He recalled the tree's words: He could take the whole pill or keep half to save a loved one's life later. He swallowed half of the pill and turned back into a human after a few minutes. Then he was heading back to the gate to return to Earth. The cave was kind of far away from the gate. He didn't care. His mind was full of Catherine—of meeting her to confess his love to her. At the end, he made it to the gate at the last minute and returned to the present time on Earth. He ran to look for Catherine. However, a sudden storm kicked up. Some huge tree branches fell down and hit Alan's head. When he was unconscious, he was being tended to in a stranger's home. Alan didn't remember his past, so the man told him to stay and treated him like his son.

***

The falling block brought all these memories back to Alan. He ran to the hospital to find Catherine.

Chapter 4

A doctor came out from the emergency room. "Who is here with Catherine Fong?" said the doctor.

"I am her friend, Alan. How is her condition now?" said Alan.

"Her condition is not stable. She sustained a severe injury to her head. I need to see whether or not her condition is stable tonight. Otherwise, her life will be in danger. She needs to be sent to the ICU. Please notify her family members at once."

"Please save Catherine. I have a lot to tell her."

"I will try my best to save her." The doctor left, and the nurses sent Catherine to ICU. Alan called Raymond to tell him about the car crash. Soon, Catherine's whole family rushed to the hospital.

After their arrival, Alan and Catherine's family were allowed to go inside the room to see Catherine during visitors' hours. Her mother asked, "What did the doctor say?"

"Her condition is unstable," said Alan in an unhappy voice. Her mother just looked at Catherine silently.

"How could this have happened?" asked her father.

"She was hit by a car on her way to see me."

"Who are you, again?"

"I—we used to be...classmates."

Her parents looked at him without saying anything and turned back to Catherine. They all looked at Catherine silently for half an hour. Then Alan asked Raymond to go out to the hall with him. They exited the room.

"I have a way to save Catherine. I recall everything now." Alan went on to tell Raymond what had happened to him in the other dimension. "I got a magic pill from the other dimension and kept half that could save her."

Raymond was shocked after hearing the story and rejected Alan's idea. Raymond said, "I only have one sister. I don't think you should be near my sister anymore. You guys have no future. Please leave now." Alan left, and Raymond returned to the room. After a while, Raymond and his parents went to the cafeteria to eat lunch. Alan saw them leave the room. He entered the room secretly. He was finally alone with Catherine. He faced Catherine, holding her hand. "Sorry that I forgot everything. I remember everything now. I left you the note because my appearance slowly turned back into a panda. I didn't want to scare you. I thought we were from two different worlds and had no future. I was able to turn back into a human after I found the magic pill from the other dimension, but then I had an accident and I forgot about everything. I will have you eat the other half of the pill. I need you to live. After you are awake, I will tell you my answer." He held her up and put the pill into her mouth, but she didn't swallow it. He got her some water and poured it into her mouth so she was able to swallow the pill.

After thirty minutes, he noticed a change in his body appearance. He was afraid that he would turn back into a panda, so he ran to the secret place to ask for help. At the same time, Catherine woke up, as her family was coming back from lunch. Her family was ecstatic. They called for the doctor, who came and had her take tests to check her brain and legs. The doctor was astonished at her quick mental and physical recovery.

"Sweetie, we are glad you are fine," said Catherine's mother.

"Yes, I am okay. Sorry to worry you guys," said Catherine. Her parents and brother left the room so that she could rest. After they left, she sneaked out of the hospital and looked around for Alan, but he was nowhere to be found. So, she returned to the hospital. She thought she'd heard what he'd said to her before and remembered that he had saved her life. However, she wasn't sure why Alan disappeared again.

Catherine was discharged from the hospital after a month. She went to the secret garden to look for Alan.

"Please come out! I know you remember everything. You saved my life, and you said you have something to tell me," said Catherine. He appeared in front of her. Their eyes met. She didn't recognize him at first. After looking carefully, she recognized his eyes. "Are you Alan?"

"Yes, are you scared of my appearance now? I totally turned back into a panda."

"No, you're still the same Alan that I met before. Please stay with me. Don't leave me again. You already left me two times."

"I know, and I'm sorry!"

"I don't want to hear 'sorry.' I just want to know; do you love me?"

"I loved you from the first time we met and will continue to love you forever."

"I love you, too."

"I won't leave you ever again. Now I am trying to look for the magic sakura tree to see if it has another way to help me turn into a human again, but I can't find it. Actually, I am kind of concerned about the tree. Its master punished it for turning me into a human."

"Well, even if you can't find it, that's fine as long as you're with me." They hugged each other and sat on the grass enjoying the scenery for a moment before setting out to look for the tree. They searched for days but couldn't find it.

One day, an old man appeared in front of them. Alan was surprised to see him there. "Shu Wei, why are you here?" asked Alan.

Catherine interrupted. "Alan, who is this person?"

"He was the one taking care of me after I lost my memories."

"I see." Catherine turned to face Shu Wei. "I can't thank you enough for taking care of Alan for so long."

Alan said, "Yup, thanks a lot. I don't know who you are but thanks for taking in a total stranger."

Shu Wei laughed. "Actually, I am not an old man. I am the tree that you guys are looking for. My master was upset with me for sending you to the dimension, so he turned me into an old man without any magic. I saw you get hit by the tree branch after taking the pill, and I decided to look after you as your guardian since you were the first one to take care of me."

"Sorry that your kindness toward me caused you trouble. You said if I didn't eat the whole pill, I could turn back into a panda any time. As you can see, I am a panda now. Are there other ways to turn me into a human again?"

"Why didn't you take the whole pill when you were at that dimension?"

"I saved the other half pill for Catherine in case something happened to her, even though you said that might have consequences."

Catherine looked at Alan, marveling at how much he'd gone through just for her. "Alan, you should have eaten the whole pill. You saved my life, and you are a panda now." Then she faced Shu Wei. "Is there anything we can do to change him back to a human?"

"I am not sure about the consequences, but it seems like Alan's accident and amnesia may be one of the pill's side effects," Shu Wei said, sighing. "It would have been easy for me to help you guys in the past, but I am powerless now. You could try to ask my master for help."

"You said you were punished by your master, so is he going to help us?" Catherine looked worried.

Suddenly, a strong wind blew the leaves away from tree. A giant fox appeared in front of them. "Master Mo!" shouted Shu Wei. "What are you doing here?"

"I knew if I didn't intervene, you would try to help them even though you have no magic," said Master Mo in a deep voice. Shu Wei didn't reply.

Alan and Catherine were shocked to see a giant fox. Alan said, "Please don't punish Shu Wei again. He is not helping us."

"I can see why Shu Wei wants to help you. You are a nice young boy. I can help you—"

"Really? You are willing to help us?" Alan cut in.

"Silence! I am not done talking yet."

"Sorry!"

"I can help you, but first you must pass my test. I need both of you to climb to the mountaintop, find a star diamond, and bring it back to me. Then, and only then, can I make you permanently human."

Catherine and Alan agreed and headed to the mountain.

"Are they going to find it? The star diamond is invisible; only the ones with power or magic are able to see it," said Shu Wei.

"Don't worry; they have the ability to see it since they swallowed the magic pill," said Master Mo.

"Still, it will be treacherous."

Catherine was nervous because she was scared of heights. Alan held both her hands. "You have me here. I will not let you get hurt again, so don't worry." After hours of climbing, they reached the top and looked high and low for the star diamond. They finally found it shining at the top of a tree. Alan climbed up the tree to get it. As they turned to go down the mountain, a ninja appeared out of nowhere. "Go down the mountain with this star diamond. I will take care of everything here," said Alan.

Catherine replied, "No, I cannot leave you unaccompanied here."

The ninja flew toward them. They just ran until they had nowhere to run, stopping to catch their breath. The ninja said, "Who are you? Give me the star diamond!"

"No," panted Alan. "We need it to pass the test."

"Unacceptable. This star diamond is to protect the whole world. It must be in this location. Otherwise, disaster will strike, and people will die."

"I don't trust you," said Catherine, still clutching the star diamond. A few moments later, images were reflected in the star diamond of many big rocks falling from the sky all over Earth, damaging countries and people. Without saying another word, Catherine and Alan handed the star diamond to the ninja, who returned it to its original spot. Then the images of the rock storm ended in the star diamond, and the ninja was gone; he'd completed his mission. Catherine and Alan went back to the secret garden without the star diamond.

Catherine said, "Sorry, we were unable to complete the mission to get the star diamond."

"Yeah, we can't live with the destruction of humanity," said Alan.

"What about you guys? Catherine, maybe you don't mind about Alan's appearance, but what about what might happen to Catherine, Alan? What if one of the side effects of being saved by the half pill is that Catherine's lifespan will be cut short? Can you live with that?" asked Master Mo.

"If we just think about our happiness and not others, we will regret it later on. We have decided to deal with our problems as they are as long as we are together. No one knows what will happen at the next moment. As long as we are happy every moment we do have, then we are satisfied," said Catherine, smiling.

"I agree with Catherine. Our love for each other is strong, so a short lifespan and a change of appearance won't affect our relationship. The important thing is that we stay together until the end."

"Well said. Congratulations, you've passed the test. Yes, getting the star diamond was the main goal, but having the heart to think about other people and the world is more important than achieving the goal. If you had brought back the star diamond knowing the consequences, then you would have failed the test." They faced each other, feeling pleased about passing the test.

Master Mo turned to Alan. "I can return you to the human form, with one limitation: You will not be a human the whole day. You will be a human during the day but turn back to a panda at night. That's all I can do." Alan nodded his head, and Master Mo completed his transition. Shu Wei was glad as he watched from the side.

Alan suddenly thought of asking for one final favor. "Master Mo, can you give power back to Shu Wei? He just wanted to help me. Please!" Master Mo was touched by Alan's compassion.

As for Catherine's short lifespan, Master Mo pulled his time machine from the sunflower and put it on the grass. "Catherine, you need to use this time machine to return to the time before you got hit by the car. Be very careful because whatever you do will change the ending between you and Alan. You only have ten hours to meet up with Alan in that dimension. I will give you a watch. You use this watch along with the time machine to come back here from that dimension. Just in case the portal closes, you still have the watch to reopen it."

"Got it," she said. Then she faced Alan. "I will find you there. This time I am sure we will be together." They hugged each other tightly, and Alan kissed Catherine's forehead to wish her good luck.

They faced Shu Wei and Master Mo. "Where are you guys going next?"

"We are going to leave here and move back to our place from far away. I will give back Shu Wei's power," answered Master Mo.

"I will follow my master," said Shu Wei. "Hope you guys live happily forever."

Alan smiled. "Take care! Thanks a lot. Hope to see you guys again. Bye!" Shu Wei and Master Mo smiled and left.

Catherine walked toward the time machine and climbed on the chair, a glass covering her as if she was inside a UFO. In an instant, Catherine and the time machine disappeared.

Catherine went back to the time when Alan was in the other dimension. She was in front of the cave waiting for Alan to come out. He was already inside the cave and had got the pill. He ate half of the pill and turned back into a human. When he exited the cave, he saw Catherine. "Alan, you left me a note. I knew something had happened to your appearance."

"Yes, Catherine, I was turned back into a panda, so I went to this dimension to get the pill. I left you a note just in case I wasn't able to return. I was about to look for you."

"Thank God nothing happened to you."

"Yup, I am fine now."

"Did you take the pill?"

"Yes, I did."

"Half pill or whole pill?"

"Half pill!"

"No, take the other half pill. You have to take the whole pill in order to stay a human forever. Don't save it to rescue me in an emergency."

"How do you know I saved the other half for you?"

"I just had a feeling that you would. Please take the other half so you can completely become a human."

"OK." He took the other half of the pill. "By the way, how did you get to this cave in this dimension?"

"Shu Wei and Master Mo sent me here by a time machine."

"I see. I have something to tell you, so listen carefully. I love you. Will you be my girlfriend?"

"Absolutely. I love you, too."

They hugged each other for a long time without noticing the time they had spent in the dimension. "Oh my God! I forgot there's a time limit to stay in this dimension. Let's use the time machine to get there to exit this dimension," said Alan.

"OK! Let's go!" They sat inside the time machine to travel to the opening of the portal. However, as they neared the portal, it was already closed.

"What should we do?" asked Alan.

"Don't worry. I have a watch that will help us to reopen the portal to go back."

"Really? Where is it?"

"Right here." Catherine noticed that it was missing. "I must have dropped it somewhere. Let's search for it."

They looked everywhere but couldn't find it. "Maybe we should go back to the cave to look for it," said Alan.

"OK, let's go."

They used the time machine to go back to the cave to look for it. After several hours of probing for it, they were tired and sat on big rocks to rest for a while. They searched for it again after they had rested. Suddenly, the cave and all the sakura trees disappeared. Catherine saw the watch on the grass after it vanished. She picked it up. "Yes, this is the watch."

"How do we activate the watch to open the portal?"

"I am not sure. Master Mo didn't say it." When she looked at the watch, it was blank. "Is it broken? It's blank."

"What should we do?"

"Are we going to stay here forever?" asked Catherine.

"I don't know, but I am sure there's a way for us to escape here. Don't worry."

"OK! I would be terrified if I were the only one here. At least we are together now."

"Yup. Now we have to figure out how to activate this watch since there are no stores that fix high-tech products. In the meantime, let's rest here." They stayed there for the night.

The next morning, the sun was quite shiny. Catherine and Alan woke up to the shiny sun. Catherine looked at the watch and saw that it was working. "Alan, look…it's working."

"Oh, yes. How?"

"Maybe this watch is a solar watch that is charged by the sun." They quickly sat inside the time machine and traveled to the entrance of the portal.

When they arrived, Catherine pointed her watch at the portal. It opened. They entered the portal right away. In an instant, they were back to the secret garden where they had first met. They hugged each other with joy.

Two months later, they entered the same high school as freshmen. They were always very sweet, making others jealous of them. They met Lillian, Sophia, and Jay again. Jay and Lillian turned out to be a perfect match. All of them attended school happily and peacefully.

Part II

Chapter 5

Alan and Catherine got married when they entered college. They'd had two cute girls: Isabelle, who was now fourteen years old, and Jamie, who was now twenty years old. The family lived happily until one day Alan and Catherine suddenly disappeared. Then the two sisters lived with their uncle, Raymond, but he often had to go on business trips, so the two sisters were often on their own. Isabelle was still in school, and Jamie worked different jobs, but they also spent time searching for their parents. They always wanted to know why their parents had disappeared. One day, Isabelle found a diary of her mother's, telling the story of another dimension, a time machine, and the secret of her father. From that day on, Isabelle was really into strange things like UFOs, aliens, and far-off planets.

Every day, Isabelle woke up at three in the morning and rushed to her desk to study. Then she dressed and went to the kitchen to cook breakfast for her sister and herself. Isabelle was aware that Jamie worked different jobs to support Isabelle and herself; therefore, Isabelle wanted to help her sister by doing the housework. "Sis, I am coming home late tonight, so you don't have to cook so much," said

Jamie. They both left the house at the same time. Isabelle walked to school, and Jamie took the bus to work.

Soon, Isabelle arrived at Pink Cherry Blossoms High School and attended her classes. During lunchtime, she would eat by herself. Unlike other teenage girls who were into fashion, she was more into books and drawing. As soon as she finished lunch, she ran to the library to study and do her homework alone. Her math teacher, Ms. Lopez, saw her at the library, so she walked over to her desk. "You are studying again. You never seem to take a break. I know you study hard, but you should relax once in a while, too. You are always getting the highest grades. We are so proud of you," said Ms. Lopez.

"Thanks for the compliment. I have no time to take a breather. I want to finish my homework soon so I can run errands and do house chores after school. I wake up every morning at three to study so it won't affect my tests and class grades," said Isabelle, looking tired.

"Wait, don't you have any adults to do housework for you? Who do you live with? You are a minor, so I have to make sure you are safe and have adults with you."

"I am currently living with my sister and uncle. My sister is an adult who is working different jobs, so I want to help her out with the housework."

"I see. Please take good care of yourself. If you need any help, let me, other teachers, and your counselor know. We will be there to support you." Ms. Lopez left the library, and Isabelle resumed doing her homework.

After school, Isabelle ran to the post office to mail a bill for her sister. Then she quickly ran to the supermarket to take advantage of the sale on tomatoes, potatoes, hams, bread, onions, eggplants, and garlic. Once home, she put the food in the refrigerator and took her dirty clothes to the basement to wash them. While she waited for the laundry to be done, she read her textbook so as to not waste any available time. She hung the clean clothes on the clothesline and cooked a noodle dish with vegetables and chicken. As soon as she finished eating, she washed the dishes and took a quick bath. She fell asleep quickly after her bath. That was basically her routine every day except weekends.

Friday was over, and Isabelle had a little free time for her hobbies. During weekends, she enjoyed going to the library to read books, especially ones about the universe. She also liked to draw in a sketchbook at the park and write in her diary. One day, she went to an antique store and saw a nice diary book, which she bought and brought home. Little did she know that the diary book was magical; whatever she wrote on the first page would come true.

That night, she wrote in her diary: "Sometimes it's boring to have the same lifestyle almost every day. I go to school, and then I do chores, run errands, study, and do homework. I want something interesting to happen in my life, like a UFO taking me to another planet or dimension. I just want a change." That weekend, she also went to the church to pray for the same thing.

Next morning, a strong wind blew outside the house, awakening Isabelle. A UFO that was shaped like a colorful mango came toward the house. It entered the balcony and shrunk to fit through the open window. When the gate door opened, an alien came out. Isabelle's jaw dropped.

Isabelle gasped. "Oh my God." The alien's appearance was shocking. His top body part was like that of a human, but his lower body part looked like a pig. Isabelle had always thought aliens were green, with big triangular heads and black eyes.

The alien introduced himself. "I am Kokochu from planet Hana, meaning planet flower, which is unknown to humans. I'm here to take you there."

Isabelle couldn't believe her dream was coming true. She thought, *Am I dreaming?* She followed Kokochu into the UFO. In a few seconds, the UFO flew out the window and returned to its original giant size. The strong wind created by the UFO disturbed some of the items in the room, and one of the photos landed in the UFO when Isabelle entered it.

They traveled through the universe at a fast speed. Isabelle looked out the window. *Wow, what a nice view!* she thought. *Am I dreaming? I can't believe I'm sitting inside this UFO with an alien. I knew UFOs existed in this world. I wonder if I can take any photographs as proof to show others later on.*

The front of the UFO looked a lot like the control panel on an airplane. The back portion was like a mini home. There were snacks, a sofa, a bookshelf with books, a computer, a coffee table, an electric stove, a toilet, a sink, a television, and a refrigerator. There were six windows, and Isabelle loved the view of the beautiful galaxy that she got from all of them.

Isabelle saw a colorful planet ahead of her. They'd arrived on the planet Hana. The planet looked different from Earth. It was like a paradise, complete with mountains and a waterfall. Everything was so colorful, like a rainbow. There were many decorated sakura trees all over the place.

The atmosphere felt like Christmastime. There were no humans living there—just half-human, half-pig aliens like Kokochu. Kokochu showed Isabelle around the neighborhood, explaining that the UFOs doubled as homes when they weren't in use for transportation. He introduced her to his friends and family members. They all welcomed Isabelle to their planet and told her to stay there as long as she wanted.

Isabelle couldn't believe what she saw. She thought, *It's like another world. There's another living planet out there. I can't believe I discovered this. This is going to be fun.* She was stunned that the aliens were friendly to outsiders, unlike people from Earth. Isabelle thought it was a peaceful planet to live on and that aliens had a simple life there.

Shortly, it was dinnertime, and Isabelle and Kokochu went to a mini mall called Aliens Sakura World. As they moved toward the restaurant, they passed an arcade center and a fortune-telling store. Isabelle was glad it was dinnertime; the day's adventures had left her incredibly hungry. Kokochu ordered leaves with white sauce. After a few minutes, their robot waiter brought over leaves on a plate. It looked so crispy like chips. Kokochu dug in and invited Isabelle to do the same. She was hesitant at first but still tried, taking one bite. It was delicious. They ended up eating the whole dish.

On their way out of the restaurant, Isabelle ran to the arcade center. Kokochu told her that all games were free to play, so she tried her hand at everything. Many of the games were similar to the arcade games on Earth, such as air hockey, dancing machine, and pinball. They ended up staying there for two hours. As they left, a mysterious guy fell down from the ceiling, collapsing in front of them.

Isabelle watched the fallen stranger for a few seconds. His skin and body features looked like those of a human's. Kokochu shook him, but he was still unconscious. He had no pulse and breath, so Isabelle did CPR. He revived, but he was still very weak, so they brought him to Kokochu's home. They put him on the sofa.

Isabelle was excited to stay in a house with an alien. She couldn't believe Kokochu had used magic eyeglasses to add more furniture and to expand the size of his home, as it was the modified version of the one he traveled to Earth in to pick up Isabelle. However, the home had no bed. Kokochu pulled out blankets from the closet, unfolded them, and spread them on the floor for Isabelle. He also gave her extra blankets in case she was cold at night. Isabelle felt it was just like the Japanese style of using a futon instead of using the bed. Kokochu put one blanket on top of the mysterious guy to keep him warm. All of them went to sleep.

In the morning, Kokochu made breakfast while Isabelle looked around the house. The mysterious guy started to move and wake up from his sleep, so Isabelle and Kokochu rushed to the sofa. When the stranger opened his eyes, he saw Isabelle and Kokochu at his side. "You're finally awake. Are you OK?" asked Isabelle worriedly.

"Yes, I am OK. Did you guys save me?" he said softly.

"Yup!"

"Thank you for saving me."

"Why did you fall down from the ceiling? Where are you from? What is your name?"

"My name is Jomo. I am from another dimension. I escaped from that dimension using my watch. My parents have disappeared. I came here to search for them."

"My parents disappeared, too," said Isabelle. "I'm looking for them. I hope we find them someday." She stopped for a moment. "How did you know this planet existed? It is unknown to the people on Earth. Even scientists don't know about it. I'm only here because Kokochu brought me here."

"My father gave me a watch and told me about the secret of the watch, which allows me to travel to another world different from the dimension. The signal of the watch directed me here."

Kokochu said, "I see. Since you have no place to go, if you don't mind, stay with us in this house until you are ready to go."

"Thank you so much." Jomo grinned. They all went to the table to eat breakfast together for the first time.

Chapter 6

Time passed by so fast. Jomo and Isabelle had been on planet Hana for three months, and they were used to their new lives. Isabelle was glad to meet Kokochu and Jomo, especially Jomo. She relished talking with him. Sometimes, they even went to the mini mall to hang out at arcade together. Very often, they went to see stars at night and observed the beautiful landscape during the day.

As happy as she was on planet Hana, Isabelle suddenly missed her happy days on Earth with her parents and Jamie. She'd recently found the family photo she'd accidentally brought into the UFO with her, and it reminded her of what she'd left behind. They'd had a good life, often going on picnics and spending time together. However, Isabelle's contented life only lasted until she was ten years old, when her parents had gone without saying a word to Isabelle and her sister. Since then, the two sisters had wondered where and why their parents had gone. They'd even called the police and family friends, but no one knew where they were. Thinking of Jamie all alone on Earth, Isabelle felt bad staying on planet Hana.

As time went by, Isabelle had developed feelings for Jomo, but she didn't confess them to him yet because she was shy and worried, he'd think she wasn't good enough for him. At the same time, Jomo had decided to reveal his own feelings to Isabelle. He wrote a letter to her asking her to meet him. Isabelle had an idea of what the meet up was about. Despite her affection for him, she felt she had no future with Jomo because of their different backgrounds, so she opted not to meet him that day. She had decided to wrap up her time on planet Hana shortly and go back to Earth to stay with Jamie and search for her parents.

Kokochu noticed Isabelle and Jomo were kind of weird without saying much to each other. Isabelle went out for a walk alone after dinner. Kokochu asked Jomo if everything was all right between them. Jomo said, "I'm meeting her tomorrow. I want to tell her I love her."

"Really? No wonder you guys didn't talk much. Good luck!" said Kokochu.

Kokochu went to clean up the room and found Isabelle's family photo on the floor. He put it on the table as Jomo walked by. Jomo was shocked by who he saw. He asked Kokochu who the woman was in the photo.

Kokochu said, "I don't know; I found it on the floor. That woman was probably Isabelle's mother." Jomo left the house without saying a word to Kokochu.

Jomo ran to a lake. Many leaves had fallen down due to the strong wind. Jomo couldn't believe that Isabelle's parents were actually his parents in the other dimension—that he and Isabelle were actually siblings. He wondered why his parents disappeared from Isabelle and from him. He flashed back to when he was still in the other dimension.

***

Jomo's first memory as a child was actually from when he was thirteen years old. He'd lost his memory of everything that had happened before then. He remembered living with his mother and father happily in the countryside.

Jomo worked at his parents' store, where they sold warm clothes. There was no electricity, so they used candles or made fires. As for the food, they purchased it from someone who shipped the food from outside their area. No one knew where the person got the food from. They also hunted for food and water from the lakes when they did thaw. Even though the living conditions were harsh, Jomo had a supportive and warm family. Everything was good until his parents disappeared all of a sudden when he was seventeen. After that, Jomo had no direction of what his future would be like. He wandered around the cold forest.

Suddenly, his high-tech watch activated, and a hole formed in front of the lake. He entered the hole in hopes that the watch was giving him a signal for finding his parents. The next thing he knew, he was being revived by Kokochu and Isabelle in the arcade.

***

Isabelle came home and saw Kokochu was watching T.V. Kokochu said, "You are finally home. Jomo went out. I heard about the meeting tomorrow. What is your answer? Not that it's any of my business; I'm just curious."

"I do have feelings for him. However, we are from two different worlds, and I've realized I need to go back to Earth to be with my sister. What kind of future could we have?" said Isabelle in a soft voice. She was miserable that Jomo wasn't home even though she decided to reject him and go back to Earth. She still wanted to see him as much as possible before her departure.

"No one knows what will happen in the future. The world may end tomorrow. The most important is appreciating the moment. You don't want to regret not taking chances in the future. Leave the fears for later. Love is a powerful thing, and I believe love solves any problems ahead of you guys as long as you have strong faith about each other's love."

"You are right. I don't know when that day will come when we have to be apart from each other, but let's worry about that when that day comes." Isabelle decided to accept Jomo's confession the next day. Jomo came home late while Isabelle was already in her room. Both Isabelle and Jomo were unable to sleep that night.

The next morning, Jomo went out early before Isabelle woke up. He didn't know how to face her. Isabelle was already at the meeting place near the largest sakura tree, waiting for Jomo. She was kind of nervous. Half an hour had passed when Jomo finally showed up in front of her. "Sorry for the wait," he said.

"It's OK. I arrived early," said Isabelle.

"I am meeting you here because I have something to ask you." Isabelle was looking forward to hearing those three words from him. Jomo continued, "I have a girl that I love a lot. I want to buy something for her. Do you know what gift to buy for a girl? She's from my dimension. I want to give it to her after I go back."

"You brought me here to tell me about the girl you love and ask me for advice on what to get her as a gift?" asked Isabelle, fighting back tears.

"Yup, we are friends, and you are a girl, so I thought you could help."

"Then why didn't you ask me at home? Why did you want to meet me here?"

Isabelle ran off crying. Jomo just stood there sadly. He couldn't tell her the truth about their relationship. He stood there for three hours, even after it started raining, remembering Isabelle's reaction.

Jomo was heartbroken. Kokochu didn't ask about their meeting, but he had an idea that it didn't work out. Isabelle wasn't home until evening. She also came home wet and collapsed in front of Kokochu. Now there were two sick people for Kokochu to take care of. Both of them stayed in bed for a week.

They finally recovered but didn't talk to each other for two weeks; they became strangers. Kokochu pretended nothing had happened but was thinking of a way to get them to talk again. One night, Kokochu made a dinner for them to join and talk. His specialties were veggie pasta, potato chips, and mango chips. The smells brought both Isabelle and Jomo to the table. Their eyes met and looked away in a second. Kokochu said, "These are the only dishes that I know how to make. Feel free to try them. I'm calling this dinner a happy friendship dinner. It is fate that all of us are here from different places to join together."

"You are right," said Isabelle with a smile.

"Yup, I agree, too," said Jomo. They started to eat and drink. Isabelle made up her mind to be Jomo's friend since she wasn't the one he loved, and she had to return to Earth soon anyway. Jomo decided to protect and support Isabelle as his sister.

Chapter 7

Everything was peaceful on planet Hana until one day, that colorful place turned dark. An evil alien king called Kingski came because he was able to sense a human on that planet. He put a spell on the aliens to control their minds. While Jomo and Kokochu were both out and Isabelle was taking a nap, Kingski captured her. By the time Jomo and Kokochu rushed home, Isabelle was gone and the home was a mess. Luckily, Kokochu had managed to avoid the mind control because he was out of the planet for an errand. Jomo wasn't affected by it because he was from another dimension, and his watch protected him. However, his watch wasn't able to locate Isabelle's location. They didn't know what to do.

Kingski put Isabelle in his mansion which looked like a church; his plan was to have her marry his son, Dano. He told his soldier to bring her to Dano's room and tell Dano that Isabelle would be his wife. Dano fell in love with Isabelle at first sight. "I heard from the soldier that you would be my wife. I'm glad," said Dano.

Isabelle was petrified and tried to escape. She shouted, "Get away from me! I don't like you. I already have someone I like. I'm only here by force." Her words hurt

Dano, but he was a very generous person and brought her to Kingski to set her free.

They went into Kingski's secret room. "Dano, what happened? Are you satisfied with that girl?" said Kingski.

Dano sadly said, "No, Dad. I will not marry her. I love her, but I don't want to force her. Why do you want us to be married?"

"I just want to create a new population. I want each of us on this planet to be half human and half alien. She's a human, so we need her. Soon, I will send my soldiers to the Earth to capture more humans. I am saving good things for you first, my son," said Kingski.

"You're selfish. You only care about yourself being powerful. That's why Mom left you," said Dano.

Kingski was mad and shouted, "I don't care whether or not you like my way of doing things. I am still your father. In order to become powerful, I need the watch for me to travel to another dimension and retrieve the sakura crystal that would allow me to control this planet and the other dimension with my creation of the new population."

Dano was disappointed at his father and just stayed quiet. Isabelle thought, *Dano is so different from his dad. I treated him with such a bad attitude earlier. I should apologize to him when I get a chance.*

Kingski was still angry and ordered his soldiers to take Dano away and lock him in his room. "Dano, sorry to put you into this mess," said Isabelle. She faced Kingski and said, "How could you treat your son like that? He's your son, you cold-blooded monster!"

"Ha ha ha, you are very brave, young girl. Do you know your position right now? You should be kneeling to beg me for forgiveness," said Kingski.

"I will find ways to save you," said Dano as soldiers came in and took him away. Then Kingski ordered another soldier to put Isabelle into a prison cell for the time being. Kingski thought, *If Dano wouldn't play along, I would marry Isabelle myself.*

How am I going to escape here? I can't even call Kokochu and Jomo. There is no cell phone here, thought Isabelle as she surveyed her prison. She saw someone's back who looked like her mother. She called out, "Mom," the woman didn't answer. She just turned her around to face her.

"Mom, it's really you. I finally found you," said Isabelle. "Why are you here? Why did you and Dad leave us? Where is Dad?"

"Sorry, I really don't know you."

"I am Isabelle, your daughter."

"I only have one son. His name is Jomo."

"Jomo? Did you just say Jomo?" asked Isabelle.

"Yes, you know him? Do you know where he is?"

Isabelle couldn't believe they were talking about the same person. "I have a friend named Jomo."

"I see. Good, he is saved."

"Why are you here?"

"I was kidnapped by Kingski. He heard from a soldier that my husband and I have a special watch to go to another dimension."

"Why does he want the watch?"

"He wants it to retrieve the sakura crystal that would allow him to control this planet and the other dimension."

Isabelle thought, *I am not sure if she is my mom or not. If she's just a lookalike, that would explain why she doesn't remember me. Otherwise, Jomo is my brother. Maybe Jomo knew about our relationship from the beginning and rejected me for that reason.*

"Where is your husband?" Isabelle asked.

"Husband? You know my husband? We are separated. I am looking for him. After I was abducted, I lost contact with him."

"Can I ask your husband's name?"

Suddenly, the lady's head hurt a lot. "I don't know why I forgot his name. Don't remember many things."

Isabelle kept silent. She had decided to trust her gut that this woman really was her mom, but pressing her for details now clearly wasn't going help her find out what had happened to her parents or what her true relationship to Jomo was.

"Why were you also kidnapped by that evil guy?" the woman asked.

"Because I am a human girl from the planet Earth. He sensed my existence on this planet, so he captured me to marry his son."

"Poor young girl! I am also a human but I am too old for him. He likes to capture teenagers."

"Oh! I didn't get a chance to ask you, what is your name?"

"I don't even remember my own name. I lost my memory when I woke up. I just remember saving Jomo and being arrested by Kingski."

"My parents disappeared. Their names are Catherine and Alan. I have a sister named Jamie."

"Sorry to hear that. I don't remember anything, so I am not sure if I am the person that you are looking for. I hope you find your parents one day."

"I hope so." Isabelle wasn't able to sleep that night. Then she recalled the story from her mother's diary about the dimension and time machine. She thought, maybe her parents really were on this planet or in the other dimension. She felt she had a chance to reunite with her mother after all.

The next day, Kingski announced to the aliens that he would marry Isabelle in three days. Isabelle heard it from soldiers who were in charge of the prison. Jomo and Kokochu heard the announcement, too. They thought for a long time of what to do next. Then Kokochu remembered he had a treasure at home that could help him to find Isabelle. Immediately, they ran home, and Kokochu searched for his magic box in the basement.

He was able to find it at last. The box was full of dust. He wiped it, and he opened the box that showed light to pinpoint her location.

As soon as they knew her spot, Kokochu and Jomo sat inside Kokochu's UFO to cross the sea. Kokochu was able to sense Isabelle strongly after crossing over the mountain.

Finally, they saw the mansion and entered. Kokochu turned them into rats so they could sneak unseen into the prison. They entered the prison and turned back into their original forms and opened the door. Isabelle was happy to see them, especially Jomo.

"How did you guys get here?" Isabelle asked.

"It's a long story. Let's escape here first and then I will tell you later when we are in a safe area," said Kokochu.

Isabelle faced Jomo, "Jomo, you have to save our...no, your mom. She is next to me in that cell."

He was surprised that Isabelle had found out about their relationship. "You already know we have the same mother?"

"Just to let you know beforehand, she forgets about many things, even me, my sister, and my dad. She still remembers you, though."

"Sorry that I didn't tell you. I saw your photo with your...our mom, and that's why we can't...you know."

"You don't have to say anything. I want to ask you their names; please tell me everything about you and them. She forgets her name and Dad's name."

"OK. Their names are Catherine and Alan." Even though she knew it was coming, Isabelle cringed at the confirmation that they were really siblings. Jomo saw her reaction. "I will tell you the rest next time. We need to get out of here quick."

From the other cell, Catherine woke up and saw Jomo. She called out, "Jomo! Is that you? It's dangerous here."

"Mom, I am all right. Good to see you. Let's leave the talking for later. We need to leave right away," he said in a rush. Isabelle just looked at them with mixed feelings. She was glad that they'd found their mother but sad that her mother had forgotten about her and Jamie. And of course, disappointed that the person of her affection was her brother.

Kokochu and Jomo rescued both Catherine and Isabelle. Kokochu had used up all his magic energy, so they had to escape in their original forms. As they left the prison, Kingski and several soldiers appeared. Jomo said, "Mom, you stay on the other side first. You, too, Isabelle. Wait for me here."

"Welcome to my mansion," said Kingski. "Allow me to introduce you to my soldiers." The soldiers marched toward them, and both sides started to fight. Dano entered and blocked the way to let the captives escape. Jomo used his magic watch to bring Kokochu, Catherine, and Isabelle to the other dimension.

Kingski saw them disappeared and realized Jomo had the magic watch. After they disappeared, he asked his soldiers to go to Earth to capture more humans. Dano said, "No, Dad, why did you do that?"

"Everything was caused by that woman who changed me. Before I met your mother, I was in love with a human girl. I happened to be on Earth at one time and met a pretty woman. It was one-sided love. She didn't like me because I told her the truth that I was an alien. She even called the police, and scientists came to capture me. Those scientists wanted to do experiments on me. That was when I began to hate humans. To become powerful, I wanted to control them. Their nice features and intelligence will help me create a new population," said Kingski.

"I didn't know you had a bad experience in the past. However, that doesn't mean you can hurt other innocent humans. You cannot assume all human beings are bad people. What you do now is wrong. Please let them go," said Dano.

"You care about them; what about me? I only have you after your mother eloped with another male human," said Kingski.

Dano said, "I didn't know Mom left because of a guy. I thought it was because you were a bad husband."

"I didn't tell you because I wanted you to remember the good side of your mother. I don't want to hurt your feelings," said Kingski. He then faced the soldiers and said, "I need you guys to go to the human world to capture more humans. Go!"

"Yes," said all the soldiers in unison. They left the mansion.

"Dad, no, please don't go any further," said Dano.

"There's no turning back," said Kingski. He left, and Dano was worried.

Jomo, Kokochu, Catherine, and Isabelle arrived to the other dimension. In that dimension, the daytime was longer than the nighttime.

Isabelle was surprised by her new surroundings. "Wow, another adventure for me. I can't believe I traveled to planet Hana and to another dimension. My life is full of adventures," she said.

Catherine said, "I know you want to look around, but we have to hurry up. I am afraid Kingski will be here soon since he is powerful. Before he comes here, we need to find the sakura crystal to control him or weaken his power. Otherwise, he will steal Jomo's watch to gain power."

Isabelle and Jomo got a bit confused. Isabelle said, "What? So, Kingski is able to enter this dimension. Since Jomo has the watch, is Jomo able to gain power?"

"Yes, when we find the sakura crystal, Jomo has to connect it with his watch to activate the power. That's why you guys have to find it as soon as possible," said Catherine.

Kokochu faced Isabelle and said, "Sorry, Isabelle; if I hadn't invited you to come to planet Hana, you wouldn't have had to go through this."

"I should say thanks to you. Without you, I'd still be living a boring life. It's always been my dream to travel to another planet and dimension. The important thing is that I met you guys and reunited with my mom even though she doesn't remember me. So, please don't blame yourself," said Isabelle.

Jomo said, "I am also glad to meet you guys on planet Hana. OK, let's look for the sakura crystal. My watch will guide us the direction."

"Let's hurry," said Isabelle.

Catherine stopped them, "Wait, I have to leave you guys to look for the sakura crystal. I have to find my husband. I have a feeling he is in this dimension."

"This place is pretty big; it won't be easy for you to find him on your own," said Jomo. "Also, we just found you. We don't want to be separated with you again."

"I just can't leave him alone. He may be in danger."

"Mom, is that your final decision?"

"Yes."

"OK, then let's make a promise. Whether or not you find Dad, we will meet at a specific location in three days. If one of us arrives before the others, we will just stay and wait until all appear. This time, we won't be separated no matter what."

"Deal! Where are we going to meet?"

"I don't think you remember our home. It's not far from here, but that place will not be found easily since it's in the countryside. How about we meet here in three days since we all know about this location?" Jomo marked a big X on the floor. "Even if we got lost, we will find each other because I will put signs wherever we go. You, too, Mom; put your signs wherever you go."

Catherine agreed.

Isabelle asked Jomo, "What is the name of this place?"

"Forever Road," answered Jomo.

Catherine said, "OK, I will remember the name of this road."

Jomo faced Catherine, "Mom, I hope you will find Dad. This time, we will meet again."

Catherine stepped forward to hug Isabelle and Jomo.

Isabelle said, "Take care! See you soon."

They waved goodbye to each other, and then Catherine went on a different path.

Chapter 8

After Catherine left, Jomo pressed the button on his watch, and the watch showed the direction of the West. They headed toward the West. After several hours, Jomo's watch had a green light flashing in front of a colorful mountain. They stopped there.

"Finally, we are here. The sakura crystal must be inside the cave since there was a door," said Isabelle. They walked toward the gate to enter the cave, but it was locked. Kokochu used his magic box to locate tools and weapons. The box showed that some tools and swords were available near an old house. So they went there, and they really found different tools and swords there. Since it was immoral to steal stuff, they put money there in exchange for the tools. Then they went back to the cave, and they used those tools to pry it open, but it wouldn't budge. Kokochu continued to figure out a way to open the door while Jomo and Isabelle checked for a back door but found nothing except a sign: "ehT NUS Si thgirb. epaCsdnAl yTtErp eht HctaW."

"Huh? What does this code mean?" asked Isabelle.

"No idea! Let's figure out the meaning of it. I guess that's the key for us to enter the cave," said Jomo.

"OK! Let's see. Some letters are in uppercase, and some letters are in lower case. You will take the lowercase letters, and I will take the upper case letters to figure it out."

"Sure! I will take the lowercase letters." They both sat on the ground to figure out the meaning of those letters. After an hour, they still had no clue.

"Wait, maybe we shouldn't do it that way. Let's change the strategy. We should work together. Let's start from the first sentence. Maybe we should try to reverse those words."

"Got it! When we reverse these words 'ehT NUS Si thgirb,' it will be 'the sun is bright.'"

"Yes, you are right. Second sentence...'epaCsdnAl yTtErp eht HctaW.' When we reverse those words, 'landscape pretty the watch,' it is 'watch the pretty landscape,' reading from last to first."

"Yup, it reads as 'the sun is bright; watch the pretty landscape.' We still have to figure out one more thing. Some of those letters are in uppercase, so let's take those uppercase letters."

"OK! T, N, U, S, S, C, A, T, E, H, and W. Let's randomly select words from here. SUN, CAT...hmmm..."

"My turn...HAT, NUT, EAT."

"The sun is bright...maybe the word is 'SUNSET' because the scenery here during sunset is pretty."

"Right! So we only have T, C, A, H, and W. Something related to the landscape. Ha! I know. It's the word 'WATCH' as appearing in the second sentence... 'watch the pretty landscape.'"

"Keywords are 'SUNSET' and 'WATCH.'"

"'WATCH' may be an object. Since there's no high technology in this dimension, I believe it is my watch that is the key to enter the cave."

"'SUNSET'? Hmmm...maybe enter the cave using your watch at sunset to activate the door to open it."

"Let's try it. It is almost sunset." They ran back to the main gate and waited until sunset.

After waiting for one hour for sunset, the watch on Jomo's hand began shaking, and a blue light shone at the door. The door opened on its own. They entered inside.

Suddenly, Kingski appeared in front of them. "Ha ha ha, thanks for showing me the way to get here and opening the door for me. It really saved me time and energy to get here." Jomo quickly gave the watch to Isabelle, and then Kokochu and Jomo started to fight with Kingski while Isabelle took off to look for the sakura crystal. Kingski tried to stop her, but he had his hands full with Jomo and Kokochu. Isabelle escaped while the three of them continued to fight.

As Isabelle followed the signal on the watch, she saw steps in front of her. She walked down the steps, and then everything turned bright. She yelled, "What's happening?"

Ten cups of green tea appeared on the floor. The words were written on the wall saying she must choose and drink one cup. There was only one cup of tea that would open the door and help her to gain power. The rest of the tea cups would lock her out. Her sixth sense and the watch guided her to drink one from the left. She picked it up and drank it. Success! A door was opened for her.

Before she entered the door, Jomo joined her. "Where's Kokochu? Did you leave him alone with Kingski?" Isabelle asked.

"Kokochu is still fighting with Kingski," said Jomo.

"You should go back. You shouldn't leave him there by himself. It's unsafe."

"He wants us to get the sakura crystal soon. He told me that he is an alien, so he knows how to handle Kingski. What's happening here?"

"It seems like we have to pass different levels here in order to get the sakura crystal. I already passed the first level."

"I see. Let's go to the next one." They entered the door to the next level.

In the second level, a ninja appeared. "You have to win against me in order to pass this level," said the ninja.

"Leave the fighting part for me," said Jomo.

"No, you can't fight alone. Actually, I gained some strength from the last level to fight."

"Really?"

"Yes, so let's face this together."

They started to move forward. Jomo only had one sword in his hand. He tried to hit the ninja, but the ninja vanished and reappeared behind them. The ninja hit them with his hand. Both fell down. Then Isabelle's watch began growing very bright, and a powerful weapon showed up. It was a crystal stick. Seeing the crystal stick made the ninja dizzy. Isabelle used it to hit the ninja's body.

Though weakened, the ninja still had some power to fight. He ordered two more ninjas to come out. Now Isabelle and Jomo were at a two-on-three disadvantage. Isabelle focused her extra strength on one of the ninjas while Jomo handled the other two. The ninjas were really powerful, and Isabelle got a punch from ninja and fell down;

however, she forced herself to stand up again. Jomo used his sword to hit the two ninjas, and then they collapsed to the floor. He saw Isabelle wasn't able to fight any further, so he assisted her with the final assailant. The ninja flew and disappeared, making it nearly impossible for them to attack him. Isabelle used her watch to guide her, and the watch showed the light up the ceiling. They looked up as the ninja jumped down, and they both used the crystal stick to vanquish him.

The gate opened, and they entered to the third level. There were one hundred ramen on the floor waiting for them. Each of them had to eat fifty bowls of ramen noodles in two hours as written on the wall.

"Well, this shouldn't be so hard. I'm a big eater, and I am super hungry, so I will be able to finish it."

She was ready to eat and said, "Itadakimasu (let's eat)." She ate nonstop from bowl one to bowl forty-nine and then slowed down in the last few minutes. Jomo had finished thirty-five bowls. The clock ticked down to only two minutes, and then she picked up the speed again. She was able to finish all her bowls. However, Jomo wasn't, so he had to stay behind to finish additional fifty bowls as punishment. Jomo told Isabelle to move on ahead without him.

She cried, "No, I can't leave you alone."

"We don't have enough time, so leave without me. Just go to the next level; I know you will make it. I will catch up with you soon. I promise."

Isabelle tried to open the door to move forward but it wouldn't open. It said once they entered the first level, they needed to pass each level together in order to proceed to the next level.

Jomo was eating his forty-ninth bowl of ramen. Isabelle joined in to help him eat some of the extra ramen bowls since she couldn't open the door. He finally started his last bowl. After they finished eating, they had a hard time moving around. They forced themselves to stand up and enter the next level.

This level instructed them to throw one hundred shrimp rolls, avocado rolls, and eel sushi rolls into the jar across the room without missing more than three times in thirty minutes. "Oh, my god, food again. At least we don't have to eat it this time," said Isabelle.

"That's true. Let's get started. Just play this as a game like we used to at the arcade center. Remember how many dolls we won that one day?"

Isabelle smiled. "Yup, let's start. *Ga yau (Do your best)*."

"*Ga yau!*"

They began throwing each roll into the jar. They took turns, throwing one by one, looking carefully at the small hole of the jar. They were thankful that they didn't have to move since they ate so much from the last level. They threw in sixty-five rolls in the first fifteen minutes, with two misses. They felt nervous. As they approached the last ten minutes, they still had twenty rolls. They were slowing down as they were worried they would fail to throw in. They had only one more chance to fail. Isabelle's hand was shaking when she threw. She missed it. They'd used up the quota of failures.

Jomo said, "You are shaking, so let me finish the rest. Rest here!"

She sat there, and Jomo went ahead to throw the last ten sushi rolls in five minutes. Soon, he only had one more to throw. He looked at Isabelle with a gentle smile and faced the jar with a serious look. Counting one, two, and three, he threw the last one. The last one fell into the jar. They hugged each other fiercely. They'd done it!

Then they looked at each other, remembering that they were siblings and that maybe they shouldn't be so close together. They were silent for couple of minutes. Then Isabelle said, "I wish time would stop at the time when we were having fun at the arcade center, but we can't go back to before. For now, we have to focus on this first."

They opened the gate to the fifth level seeing the same jar as before, but larger. It still contained all the sushi rolls but was also full of water. This level required them to drink all the water inside, without eating the sushi rolls, within thirty minutes. They were thirsty from eating all ramen, so they started to drink right away. Twenty minutes in, they'd drunk three-fourths of the water. They wanted to throw up; the water tasted so weird and disgusting. Still, they continued to drink it. Time was up, and they were able to drink all the water.

They moved quickly to the sixth level. "I am wondering how many levels we have. Don't tell me it has one hundred levels," said Jomo.

"I hope not; I am exhausted."

As they entered the gate, they only saw half of the sakura crystal in the air. They were instructed to hold two heavy water buckets—seventy pounds in total—for each person while standing. They were not allowed to move for one hour. They looked at the sakura crystal the whole time. In order to forget the heaviness of those buckets, they shifted their attention to their past when they were delighted together on planet Hana.

Their thoughts were all elated events. Jomo had recovered after falling from the ceiling. They'd lived together at Kokochu's home. They'd gone to the mall, looked at nice landscapes, used Kokochu's UFO to fly through space, and celebrated holidays with Kokochu. Thinking everyday thoughts was peaceful for them in this time of trial. Suddenly, the level's time was up, and they passed through the gate opened for them already. The sakura crystal flew through the gate ahead of them, so they followed it.

Chapter 9

The sakura crystal stopped where the other half of the sakura crystal had existed, which was in an hourglass. A fairy appeared. "I am the fairy here to protect the sakura crystal. There used to be a pill located here but your father, Alan, passed my test and got the pill. So far, you have done a great job. You must pass one more level to get this sakura crystal. Listen carefully. I will put one hundred boxes here, and a blue marble is in one of the boxes. You have only three chances in total to guess which one has the blue marble to see whether you are the owner of the sakura crystal. If you open a box with red marbles, it will explode. One more thing: You will not be allowed to open your eyes. I will use towels to cover your eyes. I will also label each box with a number from one to one hundred, so you just need to call out the number."

"Before we start the test, I want to ask you something. You said my father showed up here to get the pill a long time ago. Do you have any ideas where he might be now?" asked Isabelle.

"Yeah, I want to know, too. My mother is looking for him now," said Jomo.

"Sorry, Jomo, I have no idea where he is since he doesn't belong to this dimension. He was here as a visitor just to get the pill. But, Isabelle, I know one thing about your parents."

"Huh? What are you talking about his or my parents? We have same parents. We are brother and sister."

"No, you are a human; your parents are both human."

"Really? Then where are they?"

"They may be on Earth. I'm not sure. I just know no other humans except you and Catherine in this dimension as of now."

Isabelle felt gloomy that the parents she had been looking for all that time weren't her real parents, but she and Jomo were both relieved not to have any familial connection.

"Let's start this last level." Both were covered by a towel blocking their views. The fairy used her magic to put random marbles into some of the boxes. "You may start now."

Isabelle called out the number fifty, and the fairy opened the box. The fairy said, "No, it is not the blue marble. It is a green marble." Then, Jomo guessed the number twenty-one. The second one was also incorrect. It was a red marble. It exploded and damaged some of the other boxes.

For the final chance, Isabelle prayed and called out the number seventy, but that box was already destroyed. So, the fairy allowed them to choose one more time. They discussed which number to choose, and they whispered to each other. Jomo wanted number thirty-five, but Isabelle wanted number ninety-three. They couldn't decide, and the fairy set a time limit of one minute for them to choose a number. Counting down the minute, they both chose the number nine because that was the day when Isabelle and Jomo met each other for the first time inside the mall. The fairy opened the last box. This time, it was really a blue marble. They took off their towels and saw it.

"You passed the test. This sakura crystal is for you. Remember to put the watch around the sakura crystal to activate it," said the fairy.

The sakura crystal piece disappeared from the hourglass and appeared in the air. It combined with the other half sakura crystal and landed on Isabelle's hand. She was so thrilled. "Thanks, fairy," said Isabelle.

"You are welcome. Go back to save your friend now. Remember to put the watch around the sakura crystal. I have finished my mission here, so I am leaving now," said the fairy.

"Where are you going? Will I see you again?"

"Maybe I will see you guys someday. It was our fate to meet each other today. Take care!"

"Bye, hope to see you soon." The fairy and the cave vanished.

Kokochu and Kingski were still fighting but stopped when they saw Isabelle and Jomo. Isabelle quickly tried to put the watch around the sakura crystal, but the watch slipped from her hand and landed in front of Kingski, who quickly picked it up. He approached Isabelle to snatch the sakura crystal, but Jomo stood in front of her to protect her. Kingski batted them to the floor and turned his attention back to Isabelle. Suddenly, a panda appeared in front of him.

Isabelle was frozen with shock. The panda called out, "Isabelle, it's me, Dad. I have transformed into a panda. I met Catherine, and she asked me to run here to help you guys."

"Really? You guys met? Where is she? Does this mean she remembers everything now?"

"Yes, it's a long story. We will talk about it after I deal with this guy here. Mom is now at a safe place; don't worry."

Master Mo and the magic tree, Shu Wei also came to help. Alan said, "Why are you guys here?"

"To do what you are doing now," said Master Mo. "We came to make sure no one has full control of this dimension, the Earth, and planet Hana."

Shu Wei said, "Alan, we haven't seen each other for a long time but let's leave the talk for later."

Isabelle had no idea who the fox and tree were but figured they must be her father's allies. She'd seen so much lately that it was hard to be surprised by much anymore.

They all rushed forward to fight against Kingski. Sensing their power, Kingski transformed himself into giant alien with three clones so that it was four against four. Not to be outdone, Shu Wei transformed his crew into giant versions of themselves—everyone except Kokochu and Jomo, that is, who were still unconscious on the floor.

"Remember," said Isabelle, "we have to try to get the watch from him in order for me to activate the sakura crystal." They nodded their heads.

Each fighter focused on one of the aliens. Master Mo was fighting with the real Kingski. Alan, Isabelle, and Shu Wei fought with the three clones. They used their bare hands to hit the enemies. After an hour of fighting, Master Mo had enough. He decided to use his powerful weapon, a wooden book called Go Go Go Go Go that could move on its own. When it reached Kingski, it flew open and knocked him back to his normal size, which weakened the three clones. Alan, Isabelle, and Shu Wei were then able to take them down easily.

Master Mo took the watch from Kingski and returned it to Isabelle. As she connected it to the sakura crystal, a bright light shined on her, filling her with the power Kingski had sought and awakening Jomo and Kokochu. She felt strong. Her clothes turned into a pink dress with sakura patterns on it. She was able to fly and use her finger to put a spell on someone and used sakura petals as weapon.

Isabelle moved to put a spell on Kingski, and Dano appeared. "Please, Isabelle. I followed my father here to ask you to forgive him. He was betrayed by two women, and those betrayals of love turned into revenge," said Dano.

Isabelle said, "You're such a kind person, Dano. Sorry that I gave you an attitude when we first met. Don't worry; I'm not planning to put him to death. I just want him to go back where he came from without any power to control others."

"No, no, no!" screamed Kingski. "I'd rather die than live without power. Even if you are more powerful than me now, I still have to kill you because you are a human." He pointed his sword at Isabelle, but Dano stood in front of her, absorbing the blow. The act stunned Kingski long enough for Jomo to use his sword to stab Kingski. Bleeding, Kingski crawled to Dano and held him. "My son, Dano!

Why did you go so far for that human girl? She doesn't even love you!"

"I didn't do it for her. I did it for you. I don't want you to take revenge. You are always kind to me, but you turned into a totally different person now. I want you to turn back to your old self," said Dano.

"OK, I promise you I'll be a good person. Please don't leave me. You are the most important person to me in this world. As long as you live, we can make up for the time we've lost," said Kingski. He turned to Isabelle and begged her to save Dano.

Isabelle put a spell on both Kingski and Dano to be cured. She put a second spell on Kingski to wipe his memory of the human girl's betrayal and remove his power.

"Dano, why are we here? Where is this place?" asked Kingski.

"Oh, we are on a vacation. These people here are my friends," said Dano. The others smiled and nodded in agreement. Then Isabelle put another spell on him and Kingski to return them to planet Hana.

Alan said, "Jomo, glad to see you here, but let's leave the talk for later. We are done here. Let's go look for Catherine."

"Yes, Dad. Let's go," said Jomo.

Alan showed Jomo, Kokochu, Master Mo, Isabelle, and Shu Wei the way to where Catherine was staying. They passed through the town, which had many old, wooden houses, and took a boat across the lake to a countryside. They entered a house located near mountains full of sakura trees. Catherine was sitting on a rocking chair reading a recipe book.

"Catherine, we are back," said Alan.

"Welcome back; I'm glad to see you safe," said Catherine.

"I've missed you and Dad. Where have you been? Why did you disappear from both me and Isabelle?" asked Jomo.

"I also missed both of you. Is it true that I am not your real daughter?" added Isabelle.

Catherine told the story starting from her marriage to Alan.

***

After they got married and gave birth to a girl, they lived a happy life until their three-year-old daughter got a serious illness and passed away. They tried to look for Master Mo and Shu Wei for help, but they were nowhere to be found. They wondered whether this was one of the consequences of having eaten the pill all those years ago. Catherine was depressed for a year; she had no appetite, got skinnier each day, skipped work, and didn't get enough sleep. Even seeing a psychologist didn't help.

One day, she and Alan took a walk and saw an orphanage. Inside, she saw two cute girls who looked like their daughter. She decided to adopt them and named them Jamie and Isabelle.

Soon after adopting the two girls, Catherine was feeling better psychologically. She took good care of the two girls, helping them with homework, supporting them emotionally, spending a lot of time with them, and so on. They spent ten years together before the two girls got serious physical injuries on the same day. Isabelle's back got injured, and Jamie's legs got injured. They fell down from the escalator inside a building. Catherine prayed that if her girls recovered, she would leave them. The girls' luck changed, and Catherine and Alan felt relieved.

After Jamie and Isabelle were safely discharged from hospital, Catherine and Alan packed their belongings and asked Raymond to look after the kids since they were still young. Catherine sent them a letter explaining she would be going on a long trip with Alan.

Alan and Catherine had nowhere to go. When they were just wondering around, the secret garden appeared in front of them again. Master Mo and Shu Wei showed up. Master Mo said, "Now you see the consequences of your past actions. Your next generation is cursed, at least when it comes to blood-related and not blood-related daughters. The curse only happens to girls because, Catherine, you as a girl used the time machine to change the event in the past. Even though you've gone away in exchange for your daughters' recovery, the curse won't fade. The recovery is only temporary. To break the curse, you have to work for the other dimension to complete missions."

"What kind of missions?" asked Alan.

"I don't care; as long as our daughters are safe and free of the curse, I don't mind doing missions," said Catherine.

"Are you sure?" asked Alan.

"Yes. I can go alone. I don't want you to be in danger."

"No, I took that pill that day, and I can't leave you alone. Let's face our consequences together." Catherine cried and smiled at the same time.

Master Mo said, "Actually, to break the curse, both of you need to go to the dimension, not just one. I will send you to the dimension that you went to last time. One of the missions is to protect the dimension from danger by making sure no enemies have infiltrated it. Also, no humans should be in that dimension except Catherine. Otherwise, more troubles would be created. I will give you guys a device to detect humans' and enemies' existence. One last thing: Remember, you can't give birth to baby in that dimension because you are considered outsiders who don't belong in that dimension in the first place. You are there for your missions only."

They agreed, and Master Mo opened the gate for them to enter. Catherine turned back for a moment.

"If we are able to break the curse, I don't suppose you could bring back our oldest daughter?" she asked hopefully.

"Unfortunately, because she is already dead, there's nothing I can do about that." Catherine was saddened but resolved to do what she could to save her remaining children.

When they were in the dimension, they were assigned to a vacant house surrounded by trees, flowers, and mountains. From there on, they had to plant their own food for them and their neighbors. Their everyday activities included planting and safeguarding the dimension. They had a special device to detect any outsiders and enemies coming to the dimension. They also got the watch from Master Mo to use it in case of emergency.

There wasn't a day that they didn't think about Isabelle and Jamie—wondering how they were doing and whether they were eating well, dressing warmly, and so on. Catherine prayed for them each night.

One time while safeguarding the area, they found a young boy lying unconscious on the ground. They brought him home. When he woke up, he remembered nothing except his name, Jomo. When he saw Catherine and Alan, he called them Mom and Dad. Since he did not remember his past, she decided to take him in as her son. The curse won't happen to him as a boy, she figured, and they were doing their missions obediently.

They spent three years together. They treated him like real son. One night, Catherine heard him saying his parents' names while asleep. That's when she realized they couldn't replace his real parents. She decided to help him find his parents while on duty. They left the house for couple days, but Jomo thought they were gone forever.

Much later, after Jomo had gone to planet Hana, Catherine and Alan were still asking many creatures whether or not they know Jomo or his parents when they were in town. One of the old ladies said, "Did you just say 'Jomo?'"

"Yes, you know him?"

"Yes, I knew him and his family for a long time. They used to live in this area, but the parents passed away due to serious illness. Jomo was left alone on the street. I took him in and gave him three meals daily with a place to stay. One day he left me a note. It said, "Thank you for taking care of me. I would be fine alone." Afterward, I didn't see him. I heard a rumor that he got adopted by a couple. I guess that couple is you guys."

"Yes, we took him in as a son. We lived together for several years, but now we can't find him."

"I see. I will ask around; others here may have seen him. If I find him, I will let you guys know."

Of course, they didn't find Jomo. Alan and Catherine went home. Alan saw her anxious face, and he comforted her. Then he went to the kitchen to cook for her. When he came out, Catherine was gone. She'd gone out to look for Jomo. Near the lake, she found an old book that had belonged to Jomo. She worried he may be in danger, so she jumped into the lake.

She didn't find him, but in the process, she entered the gate to planet Hana, where she landed in the grass near Kingski's mansion. Kingski's soldiers found her and took her to him. Kingski sensed she was a human who may have the magic watch, so he put her in prison. That was when Catherine met Isabelle again. It was all she could do to pretend she didn't recognize her own daughter for fear of the curse.

***

Catherine finished telling the story. "Mom, you left me because you were helping me to find my parents," said Jomo. "Why didn't you tell me?"

"I left a note in the house that we would be out for several days."

"I didn't see it. I rushed out to search for you guys without looking at anything else in the house. Sorry, I thought you guys didn't want me."

"What happened to you afterward? We didn't see you when we returned home. We were looking all over the area for you."

"Oh, I thought you guys had disappeared, so I walked around to find you guys. I saw my watch was signaling near the lake, so I just followed the way. I thought the watch was telling me where you and Dad were, so I jumped into the lake and entered planet Hana, where I met Isabelle and Kokochu." He paused. "I don't remember my past of my real parents. I just remember you and Dad living happily with me. Are you still going to accept me even though I am not your real son?"

Catherine hugged Jomo and cried out, "Of course, you are my son forever. Hmmm... sorry, we felt bad to find out that your parents had passed away."

He grinned and said, "I am fine, Mom." He appeared fine, but Catherine knew he was hiding his sadness from everyone.

Then Catherine faced Isabelle, "I'm so sorry to have left you and Jamie. Dad and I had our reasons, but we have been thinking of you guys every day and night, praying you guys are safe. It was so hard to pretend not to know you in the prison. At that moment, I wanted to hug you."

Isabelle said, "That's OK, Mom. I'm pleased that you didn't forget about us."

Isabelle looked at her father and her mother, and then three of them hugged each other.

Isabelle asked, "Dad, where did you find Mom after we entered the cave? How come Shu Wei and Master Mo were with you?"

"I found Catherine at an old wooden house. I have a device to detect humans' existence in this dimension. My device sensed a human there, so I walked there to take a look, and that was when I found her. She told me everything about you guys. I told her to stay in the house to wait for us. Then I went to Earth to ask for Master Mo and Shu Wei to help me. I promised them that I would do more missions in exchange for the safety of Jomo, Catherine, Jamie, and you."

"Ah, that makes sense."

"One thing we couldn't believe was you and Jomo not only met but also fell in love. Sorry that the sibling confusion caused you guys so much pain."

Jomo and Isabelle were happy and embraced each other.

"Are you all coming back to Earth with us?" asked Isabelle.

"Sorry, we have to complete missions here to free the curse, and I don't want anything to happen to you and Jamie when we are together."

"I don't care about the curse. I don't want to be apart from you and Dad. Let's face the curse together. Maybe I can use my new powers to free the curse."

"No, don't do that. We have to be responsible for what we did. I used the time machine to change past events, and your dad took the magic pill to change his appearance and to save me. We don't regret it. At least we are together now. It's just that we have to complete missions as our punishment. I promise all of us will meet someday when the curse is gone."

"OK, I respect your decision. As long as you and Dad are safe, then Jamie, Jomo, and I will be happy." Catherine and Alan beamed.

Master Mo stepped forward, "Shu Wei and I will return to our home. I will leave things for the young generation to take care of. They are capable of dealing with issues. That's how they grow. I have confident for them. Lastly, I wish now that the curse hadn't been so strong."

"It's OK. It's not your problem. We should accept the consequence of what we did."

Shu Wei said, "I will continue to find ways to help both of you. I want a happy ending."

Catherine gave a good luck charm to Isabelle and Jomo. Alan and Catherine watched the others jump into the lake and through the portal to planet Hana.

Chapter 10

In an instant, they were back at Kingski's mansion. Dano had already brought all the aliens to the mansion. Isabelle put a spell on the alien population to rid them of Kingski's mind control. Then Dano told Isabelle that soldiers had already gone to Earth to capture humans, and she needed to hurry to save the human world.

"Oh, I didn't know about that. Let's quickly go to Earth now," said Isabelle.

Dano told Isabelle and Jomo to go ahead without him because he was still searching for the stone and stamp from his father that would allow him the royal power to stop those soldiers. Kingski had forgotten where he had put the stone and stamp. They agreed and left the mansion.

Soon Isabelle, Jomo, Kokochu, and the aliens arrived on Earth to save the people. Isabelle feared the carnage that might be coming. The soldiers destroyed the city. The destruction was incredible. The soldiers herded the humans into UFOs. Isabelle seemed to be losing her power because she had used too much power before and had no power when she was out of planet Hana and the dimension. Isabelle and Jomo felt powerless and frustrated that they couldn't do anything. However, they still had the aliens and

Kokochu. They outnumbered the soldiers as they had the benefit of using special silver sticks that blew poisonous colorful bubbles of smoke at the soldiers.

Still, the soldiers put up quite a fight. Right on time, Dano stood in front of them and ordered the soldiers to stop immediately. "My father, Kingski, is no longer the king. He has retired, and I will be replacing him. This is the stamp and stone given to me by my father," said Dano.

When the soldiers saw it, they dropped their weapons and kneeled down. They said, "Our new king, Dano." They listened to Dano's order to stop the fight.

"Free the people and return to planet Hana right now."

"Yes, my king," answered all the soldiers.

It was over. Isabelle stood motionless. She hadn't been on Earth for a long time. Jomo walked over and tapped her shoulder. "Have you decided whether you're staying here or go back?" he asked.

"I don't know. I still have family here. I can't leave them alone. It would be selfish of me to think only of myself. But at the same time, I don't want to be separated from you," said Isabelle.

"I wish I could stay here but, as you already know, I can't."

"I understand. That's why it's so hard for me to choose whether or not to go back."

"Go by your heart. I will respect your choice."

She thought for a moment. "OK, I will go back with you for a while. But I want to see my sister first. By the way, what should we do for the city to return back to the original condition? Look at the mess here." They all looked around the city. Dano saw Isabelle's troubled face and ordered the soldiers to restore the city to the original state. They listened and went ahead to rebuild the city. The other aliens also helped them to speed up the process. Isabelle felt relieved and returned home secretly to look at Jamie at home alone. Afterward, they all went back to planet Hana except the soldiers and aliens who needed to stay on Earth until the city was back to normal. The humans, who were rescued by the aliens asked polices to assist them with the recovery of the city.

Isabelle stayed on planet Hana for a week until one day during dinner with everyone, when she suddenly fell to the floor due to using the magic spells so many times. Kokochu and Dano hurried over, and Jomo held her up. "What happen?" said Jomo.

"I used too much power. The fairy secretly gave me a paper note inside a mini blue bag when you weren't aware of. The note stated: Be careful of using the power. If you used too much, you would disappear or die." Isabelle continued, "I had no choice at that time because I had to save everyone. I already saw my parents, my sister, and you guys, so I have no regrets. I am glad I was able to help you without causing you trouble. The fairy also told me that you'd have to return to your dimension after everything was resolved. If you don't return, you will die because you don't belong to this planet or the Earth. I've stayed here for a while because I want to have good memories with you and Kokochu before you return to your dimension," said Isabelle.

Jomo said, "I don't care about my life. I live for you." He turned to Kokochu. "Is there a way to save her?"

Kokochu sighed. "I can't think of one. I wish I could."

Suddenly, the fairy appeared in front of them. "You are such a good girl. You think about others before yourself. I will save you. To save you, you have to return the sakura crystal to where it belongs. This way, you will be the same old Isabelle. So Jomo has to bring this sakura crystal back to his dimension, and he has to stay in that dimension to keep him alive." Jomo and Isabelle looked at each other sadly.

Jomo said, "OK, as long as she stays alive, I don't mind bringing it back. However, I will return to look for her," said Jomo.

"No, you have to stay in your dimension. Otherwise, you will die," said Isabelle.

"OK, I promise I will stay in that dimension, but you have to stay alive and healthy, too."

"As long as we are both alive, I'm sure there's a way for us to meet again someday. I am happy that I am in love with you. So many great experiences and adventures happened after I met you."

"I love you! Let's meet again," said Jomo miserably. They cried and hugged each other one last time before departure.

The fairy said, "I hope both of you meet again someday."

Jomo and Isabelle said, "Thanks! We will wait for that day to come." Jomo took the sakura crystal and used his watch to enter the dimension with the fairy.

Soon, Isabelle recovered from her illness and decided to go back to Earth. The day she left, Dano sent her off. "Thank you for everything, Dano. You've always been a good friend to me even though I can't return your love," said Isabelle.

"It's OK. I have my own way of loving you. As long as you stay healthy and happy, then I'm happy. I will continue to love you until I find my other half. Right now, I want to spend more time with my father to make up for the past. Take good care of yourself. Don't forget about us. Hope you see Jomo soon," said Dano.

Isabelle smiled and said, "Thanks. I hope you find the other half soon. I know you will find a wonderful lady who will love you very much. Take care! Bye."

"Bye," said Dano.

Kokochu sent Isabelle back to Earth using his UFO. "Kokochu, thanks for everything. You were the first friend I met on planet Hana. I am glad I met you. This adventure has been more than I ever could have imagined," said Isabelle.

Kokochu said, "Please don't make me cry. I am going to miss you. Don't forget about me. I will try my best to find out a way for you and Jomo to meet. Hopefully, you will see your parents soon. I will come visit you once in a while. So next time, don't be surprised at seeing a UFO or me." They both laughed and then cried. They arrived on Earth in front of Isabelle's home. Then Kokochu left, and Isabelle saw the UFO disappeared from the sky.

Isabelle went inside and hugged Jamie right away. Jamie said, "Where have you been? I called the police. I was so worried. I thought something happened to you. You are not the kind of person who disappears suddenly without saying a word to me." Isabelle told Jamie about the whole adventure. That night, both of them talked and ate dinner together. Afterward, Isabelle went back to her room and looked out the window, wondering what Jomo and the others were doing. Then, she looked at her clean room. Jamie kept the room very neat and clean. Before she fell asleep, she recorded her adventure in her diary.

Chapter 11

Four years passed; Isabelle graduated from high school with honors. Soon Isabelle was ready for her first year of college. As usual, she was focused in all her classes and was excited about college life. She explored the college environment, especially the library. She rushed to the library, and she was amazed by what she saw there. There were more than seven floors and each floor was huge.

After school, she went home and saw someone standing in front of her house. It was Jomo. Isabelle was too thrilled. They embraced each other. Then Isabelle said, "How did you get here? Is it OK for you to be on Earth? I thought we agreed you'd stay in the dimension so you wouldn't die."

"Kokochu brought me here. Don't worry, I won't die. Three months ago, I got hit by lightning. I was in a coma until the fairy used magic to help me to recover my consciousness and past memories, although I still don't remember my parents' faces. After I regained most of my memories, I went to visit my parents' friend. Their friend told me everything about what had happened to me. I made a mistake. I am actually not from that dimension. My parents and I were kidnapped and taken to that dimension when I was still an infant. We are all humans, but I am not sure why I am able to live in that dimension as a human," said Jomo.

"Oh, wow. I see. I'm glad you are back. Where's Kokochu?" asked Isabelle.

"Kokochu is still on Earth, running errands," said Jomo.

"I am so glad to see you again. I've missed you, Jomo."

"Me, too. I'm happy that we can be together again and that we are not siblings. I am lucky to have you and our adoptive parents. I should call them Father-in-law and Mother-in-law in the future."

Isabelle blushed and turned away. "Who said I'd marry you? I have many other choices in college."

"They won't get a chance to beat me because you only love me, and I also love you."

"Boy, somebody's pretty confident."

Jomo kissed her directly. That was their first kiss. They were both embarrassed.

"By the way, did you wait long for me here?" asked Isabelle.

"I didn't wait long. I only waited for several hours. I wanted to see you as soon as possible, so I came here early—but you'd already gone to school. Actually, I have a surprise for you," said Jomo.

"Of course, I'd already gone to school. It is my first— wait…surprise? What surprise?"

"Let's go in the house. They are waiting for you now."

"Who? Is it Mom and Dad? Have they returned to Earth?"

"Yup! They tried very hard to complete the number of missions as soon as possible just to see you, Jamie, and, of course, me. As for the curse, they made an agreement that lets them return once a year to Earth for a couple of months as long as they can go back to the dimension to continue taking on missions. They'll have new missions every year. They've completed the one for this year."

"Who did they make a promise to break the curse?"

"I am not sure, but they mentioned the top or highest creature in the dimension. Master Mo brought them to that authority to negotiate to break the curse."

"I see."

Isabelle called Jamie to come home right away. Then Isabelle and Jomo rushed into the house. "Mom, Dad, you guys are back. Welcome home!"

Catherine rushed over to hug Isabelle. "Good to see you again. It's always nice seeing you healthy and well."

Alan walked over. "Welcome home! We already made dinner for you, Jamie, and Jomo."

Jamie opened the door, and they all said, "Welcome home, Jamie." Jamie was surprised and happy to see them. She hugged both Catherine and Alan.

"Mom, Dad, welcome home! Isabelle told me everything. From now on, we are going to stay together forever."

"Unfortunately, we have to leave in a few months. We promised the authority in that dimension that we'd complete a number of missions each year in order to see you guys," said Alan.

"Well, a couple of months are better than none. At least we can celebrate the New Year together."

"I am thinking maybe next year Mom will come here from January to March, and I will stay here from March to May. This way, you guys can stay three months with me and three months with her, with one month of us all staying together. What do you guys think?"

"Good idea! That would only leave us six months alone. We are now independent as well as supportive of each other."

Jamie then faced Jomo. "Oh, by the way, you must be Jomo, the guy who loves my sister a lot. I heard a lot about you from my sister. You are also our parents' adoptive son. Do you prefer to think of them as Mom and Dad or Mother-in-law and Father-in-law in the future?"

Isabelle's face turned red. "Hey, sister, why did you bring that up so suddenly?"

"Oh, don't be shy. I know you want to marry him," said Jamie.

Catherine laughed and said, "Jamie, don't tease your sister so much."

"Actually, I like Mother-in-law and Father-in-law more than just Mom and Dad," said Jomo.

Everyone laughed.

"I can't believe we're still talking about this," said Isabelle.

"When are you guys planning to marry?" asked Catherine.

"As soon as possible," said Jomo with a serious face.

"You didn't propose marriage to me. I want a romantic proposal before I marry you, and I won't marry you until after I complete college."

"OK, agreed!"

"Also, you can move here to live with me, but you will sleep in a separate room. This way, we have more time to see each other, and it saves you a lot of money."

"OK, Wife."

"I am not your wife yet."

That night they had the best dinner, laughing and talking all evening.

The next day, Isabelle had no school, so Isabelle and Jomo went on a date at the park, and then they went to watch a movie.

That night, Isabelle returned home with Jomo to wait for Kokochu to show up. Finally, he showed up, entering through the window. Isabelle was so happy to see Kokochu again. She punched him and said, "You didn't even visit me once after I returned to Earth."

"Oh, I was too busy before, but I knew you were doing fine. I have a spy plane to watch you. I came now because I really want a happy reunion of all three of us together," said Kokochu. They talked the whole night.

After a few months, Kokochu went back to planet Hana. Catherine and Alan also returned to the dimension. Jomo, Isabelle, and Jamie lived together under the same roof. Isabelle continued to attend college, and Jomo took the GED to prepare to enter college himself. Jomo and Isabelle also worked part time together at a café, while Jamie got promoted as a supervisor at her agency. They all lived a peaceful life, waiting and looking forward to the next family reunion.

Part III

Chapter 12

"Jomo, wake up! Don't be a lazy pig. It's time for work," scouted Isabelle.

"Yes, my wife. Let me sleep for five more minutes."

"Alright, last five minutes," sighed Isabelle.

Isabelle entered another room where her daughter, Jennifer was at.

"You better wake up for school. You're gonna be late like your dad. Hurry up!" yelled Isabelle.

"OK! OK! Give me one more minute. I promise," said Jennifer with her eyes closed.

Isabelle said, "Like father like daughter...No, I can't spoil you like that. You need to wake up now." Isabelle dragged her to the bathroom. "Here you go. Go get ready and come down to have breakfast." Isabelle rushed back to her room to wake up Jomo. This time, Jomo woke up and got dressed.

Soon, they sat down to have breakfast together.

"Good morning, Dad and Mom."

"Good morning, Jennifer," said Isabelle and Jomo.

After they had breakfast, they left the house with only Isabelle at home who was a full-time housewife. She left her last job after she gave birth to Jennifer. Jomo was working as a high school teacher. Jennifer was attending high school in her senior year.

Jennifer arrived at school. She was busy chatting with her friends in class. Her teacher, Mr. Wong came over and asked her, "Where's your homework for last week and today? I need to talk to your parents about your performance."

"No, one more chance please. I will hand in the homework tomorrow."

"OK, one more chance. I need to see it at the beginning of the class tomorrow. Got it?"

"Yes, I promise I will have it ready by tomorrow." Mr. Wong walked back to the whiteboard to start his lesson.

As soon as the class ended, Jennifer rushed to the library to search for books about robots and astronomy. She wanted to know more about it and wished to have her adventures like her parents and grandparents. "Life is just too boring now. When do I have my own adventure?" asked herself.

After school, she walked to different stores randomly. She saw a shop called D. Perfect Robots that sell robots. She walked into the shop. She saw many robot toys but she had no interest in them. She asked the owner, "None of them look like humans. Do you have any more hidden away?"

The owner said, "You can order it on our computer for high-tech robots that look like human, but it costs a lot of money. You look like a student, so I don't think you can afford it."

"How much?"

"Nine million dollars."

"What? Too expensive. Could you show me some samples to prove that it is worth the price?"

The owner asked his wife to watch the shop and asked Jennifer to follow her. She followed him to a room and then passed another hallway to get into another room in a dim light. She saw a room full of high technologies like a science lab. The owner turned on the screen. "Are you ready to see my robots?"

"Yes. Go ahead and show me." The owner pressed the remote control and all the robots appeared on screen.

"OMG, they really look like humans. No wonder it's so expensive. How many have you sold out?"

"None. Because this is the first time a customer has asked me about humanoid robots."

"Could you lower the price?"

"Even if I lower it, it will still be expensive for you as a student."

"True."

"However, you can work here part time as my employee with minimum wages and use our robots for only one hour each day during your break time."

"Sure, but why do you allow me to work here?"

"I guess it's fate."

"I see. By the way, my name is Jennifer. What's your name?"

"Daniel, the scientist who created these robots."

"Wow, impressive."

"Could I try it now?"

"Sure."

Daniel pressed the button, and a robot was activated to walk out from the closet.

"Hi. I am Robot #1."

"Hi. I am Jennifer."

The robot recorded Jennifer's name into its machine.

"Hi, Jennifer. Nice to meet you."

"Wow, you really look like a human. You have a girly face like Korean boys. You are my type."

"Thanks."

"What's your name?"

"You can call me any name you want?"

"How about Frankie?"

"OK, I am Frankie from now on."

Jennifer couldn't take her eyes off Frankie. It was love at first sight. Jennifer and Frankie went outside for a walk. No one noticed that Frankie was a robot. It looked more like a male model. The girls looked at Frankie, and Jennifer got mad. Frankie saw her reaction; it went to pick up a sakura from a tree and gave it to her.

"Don't be mad."

"No, I am not."

"Yes, you are. I could see it."

"Yes, yes, you know because you are a robot."

"Why are you mad?"

"Nothing! Forgive you this time since it's not your fault that you look so handsome."

Frankie smiled warmly. Then, they returned to the shop. Daniel pressed the shutdown button and charged Frankie. It stopped moving and talking.

Jennifer left the shop and took the bus home.

"How was school today?" asked Isabelle, happily cooking in the kitchen.

"Good. Mom, I found a job at a shop that sells robots."

"What? Why all of a sudden? You don't have to worry about money. I just need you to focus on your academics."

"I will still go to school. Plus, I only work part time there."

"I said no. Absolutely no."

"I already decided it."

"You are still a minor. I won't sign the paperwork."

"I hate you. I am leaving this house." Jennifer was angry and ran out of the house. Isabelle was upset and sat at the chair looking at the food silently. Then, her tears were dripping down to the food.

Jennifer kept on running until she reached the shop. Jennifer entered the shop. Daniel's wife was cleaning the shop.

"Hi, welcome, Jennifer."

"Hi, you are...?"

"Kimberly, Daniel's wife. Daniel is inside his lab. Why are you here at this hour? It is getting late now. You should go home."

"I have nowhere to go. My mom is not allowing me to work."

"I see. Come stay with us for a while, and we will send you home later."

"Thanks."

Kimberly closed the shop and walked to the lab room with Jennifer.

On the other hand, Isabelle was so scared and worried about her not returning home yet. Jomo came home after receiving Isabelle's call.

"What should I do now? Should I call the police?"

"It's not twenty-four hours yet. I can locate her location. I put GPS on her phone just in case."

"Where is she now?"

Jomo tracked Jennifer's location. He found it. They rushed out of the house right away without bringing any of their belongings.

Soon, Isabelle and Jomo arrived at the shop but it was closed. They knocked at the door, no one answered but they saw the light was on inside the room.

"I believe she is inside with the owner. We will wait here until she comes out," said Jomo.

"Yup."

They waited outside for an hour but Jennifer was still not out yet. Then, they saw the light was off. Jomo checked the GPS again; he saw the GPS wasn't at the shop. The GPS signal was off. They were starting to get fearful and broke the door to go in the shop. They entered the room but no one was there.

"Wait, there's another door here," said Isabelle.

"Let's go in and check it out."

They entered the door and passed the hallway to another room which was the science lab.

"What is this? A lab with all robots?"

"I have a bad feeling about it. I think Jennifer has disappeared here to somewhere…another dimension, another world, to the past or to the future."

"We need to continue to search here to find the path there."

They searched all over the place but had no hint of how to get there.

"I shouldn't have let her go, I shouldn't have let her go, I shouldn't have let her go, I should have gone after her. What should we do now?" cried Isabelle.

"Don't blame yourself. We went through a lot in the past, and look at us. We are together now."

Jomo went ahead to hug Isabelle. She was crying a lot. When she stopped crying, they continued to search for hints in the lab. They had a feeling that Jennifer disappeared from there. Isabelle started to get frustrated and panic, so she started to press any button to see if there was any hope. Isabelle accidentally pressed the button and activated a portal connecting to another world. However, it required a password to access it. They had no idea of the password.

"What should we do? We don't know anything about the owner," said Isabelle.

"Let's see. This shop is D. Perfect Robots. Maybe try it backward like stobortcefrepd." Isabelle typed in the password, and it was incorrect. "Isabelle, let's try stobortcefrepd10 since there are ten human-like robots here."

Isabelle typed it in, and the system showed 'WRONG.'

"One last chance. Let's think."

Chapter 13

Jennifer, Daniel, Kimberly, and Frankie exited the portal to another world.

"Where am I? We just exited the black portal. It looks like black hole," said Jennifer.

"It's not a black hole, but another dimension called Ever Sakura dimension."

"Why did you bring me here?"

"We know your parents and grandparents went to the other dimension before, so we need their help to find our son who had gone missing there," said Daniel. Kimberly nodded her head.

"How did you know so much about my family? Is that why you hired me to work at your shop?"

"Yup. Sorry that we have used you. This is the only way we could get close to you and your parents. I am sure when they know we have kidnapped you, they would find a way to come here."

"You!"

"We won't hurt you. Please help us!"

"Fine! Finally, I have my own adventure. How do you know that my parents and grandparents are able to help you find your son?"

"I heard that your grandparents, Catherine and Alan are protecting this dimension, so I think they may have a connection here to find our son. This is our only hope. We lost our son here a long time ago."

"I see. OK, I have decided to help both of you to find your son. Do you think my parents are able to travel here and know I am here?"

"I put some hints there, so I am sure they will find it."

"Oh, I hope they find it, but why do you make it so complicated for them over there?"

"Because my shop never existed in the first place. I made it only available to you and your parents. Other people don't see it. I have created my robots, so I don't want to take the risk for the shop to be taken away by the evils who find out about our shop. I trust you and your family. Anyway, when they activate the portal, the shop will disappear by itself and it will turn into a rainbow necklace."

"I see." They waited under the sakura tree.

On the other hand, Isabelle and Jomo were still searching for hints. While searching, they found a picture of Daniel, Kimberly and the robots with words printed at robots. It printed, 'missingson.' The picture was upside down and had ten robots but with eight next to Daniel and two next to Kimberly.

"Maybe it's 8nosgnissim2."

Isabelle typed it into the system, and it worked. The shop was shaking and turned into a rainbow necklace. Then, the dark portal opened. They took the rainbow necklace and entered the portal. Through the tunnel, they saw two paths to the dimension.

"Which one to go into?" asked Isabelle.

"I am not sure. It wasn't like this before. Weird."

"How about you go that way, and I go this way? At least one of us will find Jennifer."

"If we missed this chance, I don't know how we would go the other way."

"Don't worry, I am sure we will meet again. We went through a lot together."

They travelled different ways, and it took a long time to reach the dimension.

Isabelle arrived at the dimension.

"We are back here again. Haven't been here for a long time. Oh, yeah, Jomo is not with me now."

She walked around the area to look for Jennifer but she was nowhere to be found. She then walked to Catherine and Alan's home to seek help from them.

"Mom, Dad!"

"Isabelle!"

Catherine and Alan hugged Isabelle tightly with tears dripping down like rain pouring down from the sky. Isabelle also cried.

"Isabelle, did something happen?" asked Catherine.

"Yes, Jennifer is missing. She got kidnapped by the owner of the shop that sells robots. Jomo went into a different path in the portal to look for Jennifer. I am a bad mom. We had an argument. I shouldn't have let her leave the home."

"Don't worry! Alan and I will find Jennifer."

"Do you know anything about the owner?" asked Alan.

"Not much, never seen him. Just saw the shop, the lab, and the picture of the owner, a lady and those robots. When the portal opened, it's weird to see the shop vanished and turned into a rainbow necklace."

"Rainbow necklace? Show me!"

Isabelle showed it to her parents. They looked at it carefully and found a little GPS detector.

"Why does the owner have a GPS detector inside the rainbow necklace? Maybe the owner wants you and Jomo to find their location. If it's really kidnapping, the owner won't put a GPS detector and allow you guys to easily find them."

"True," nodded Isabelle and Alan.

"Let me try to put this GPS detector into my new invention of the highest technology in this dimension to do different functions like a smartphone. Since we don't have smartphones here, I made this. Your cellular phone from Earth has no signal here."

"Yeah, I know."

Catherine plotted the GPS detector into the system. The screen was on detecting their location.

"Found them."

"Where?" asked Isabelle.

"Near the sakura trees. Let's go."

They left the house and rushed over to the location.

Soon, they arrived at the location and saw them sitting under the sakura tree waiting for them. Isabelle rushed over to Jennifer.

"I finally found you, Jennifer. Are you OK? Did they do anything to you? Are you hurt somewhere?"

"Mom, I am totally fine. Sorry for running away from home."

"I am glad you are fine."

They hugged each other. Then, Jennifer faced her grandparents. "Wow, I haven't seen grandma and grandpa for a long time. Plus, this is my first time travelling to another dimension to see grandma and grandpa. My adventure!"

"Oh, my granddaughter, you grew taller," said Alan.

"Yup, so pleased to see you here," said Catherine.

Isabelle turned and faced Daniel, Kimberly, and Frankie.

"Why did you have kidnapped my daughter? What do you need?"

"I have no other way but to do that. Please let me tell you the whole story, and you can decide whether or not to help us," said Daniel in a soft voice.

"Say it."

"Many years ago, my son, my wife and I lived happily on Earth. Until one day, aliens came to kidnap us to this dimension for an experiment to study human beings and make clones using a clone machine in order to control them for future weapons against the people on Earth. That was what I heard from the alien. We tried very hard to escape from them, but we were not able to return to Earth. Not that I found a way at that time. We had no choice but to live here. While living here, we got a serious disease but thank god my son was fine. So, I gave my son to my friend that we met here to look after him. We were lucky to find the herb to cure our disease. After that, it took us some time to totally recover. As soon as we felt better, I went to my friend's home, but they went missing."

"But why do you need us here?" asked Isabelle.

"I heard about your story and your parents' story, so I feel like you guys have the power to help me find my son."

"How could you be so sure? You should tell us at the beginning. You are like gambling to see whether or not we would be able to make it here."

"To be safe, I put a GPS detector into a rainbow necklace after you activated the system."

"How did you return to Earth in the past?"

"I think it has to do with this rainbow necklace that connects the Earth to this dimension. After we have this rainbow necklace, we have a special power to make objects smaller."

"I see. We will help you," said Catherine.

"How does your son look like? Any characteristics or marks?" asked Isabelle.

"He has a mark that looks like sakura on his back."

"Wait? Sakura mark on back?"

"Yes."

"What a coincidence! My husband has a sakura mark on his back. Also, he told me the story of his past that is similar to yours."

"Really? Where is he right now?"

"Where's my son?" asked Kimberly.

"We went different paths on our way here. There were two paths so we went different ways."

"Oh, no! He shouldn't use the other path. Actually, we gave you guys a hint of which path to enter. The picture you saw was on the right side of the door and not on the left side."

"What? That's a hint? We focused too much on the hints in the picture for the password...but what's on the left side of the path?"

"Danger! It is a path to another dark dimension, where lives the evil chubby queen and her robots. They capture humans to become her slaves and then study them to make perfect robots like human's brains and figures."

"How do you know all about their motive?"

"I overheard one of the robots telling another robot about that. Not sure if it's true."

Isabelle was scared after hearing that. "We shouldn't have gone different ways. What has happened to me? I have made wrong choices recently."

"It is not the time to blame yourself but to figure out a solution. We went through a lot in the past so nothing scared us anymore. So, just calm down to see what we could do," said Catherine. She turned away from Isabelle and faced Daniel and Kimberly.

"Do you have a way to go to the dark dimension?"

"Not so sure. We were only there for one time by mistake, but they didn't see us," said Daniel.

"Just recall anything from that time that led both of you there. Any little things may be helpful for us to find the link to that dimension."

"Hmmm...let me think."

"Oh, blood dropped on the rainbow necklace under the bright sun," said Kimberly.

"Whose blood?"

"Daniel got a cut on his hand, so it was his blood."

"What else?"

"It was in May."

"OK. Did you see two paths when you came here this time?"

"No. I don't know why Isabelle and my son saw two paths."

Catherine turned around and asked Isabelle, "Is there anything that you could recall before entering the portal and during your travel in the portal?"

"Let's see...rain, evening time, the rainbow necklace, and Jomo's blood."

"How much Jomo was bleeding at that time?"

"Oh, it was a minor scratch that he accidentally did on himself."

"So, the blood got on the rainbow necklace?"

"Yes."

"Maybe Jomo and Daniel are blood-related. They happened to have blood on the necklace that opens the dark dimension. I assume other people's blood on the rainbow necklace can't open the dark dimension. There is nothing to do with the weather and time since they entered during sunny day in May and you two entered during evening and rainy day in March."

"I see."

Catherine faced Daniel, "Do you know why you have a connection to the dark dimension? In other words, why only your blood and Jomo's blood?"

"I am not sure. I want to know the answer, too. Why only us and not others? I am wondering what we have to do with the other world."

"For my understanding, Jomo is just a human," said Isabelle.

"Yup, Kimberly and I are both human."

"Anyway, we shouldn't worry about this now. Let's go to the dark dimension now," said Catherine.

They waited for Daniel to activate the portal. Daniel used a knife to cut a little bit of his left index finger and put a drop on the rainbow necklace. The hole to the portal opened little by little, then all of them entered the portal.

Chapter 14

Soon, they exited the only path to the dark dimension. Over there, the sky was cloudy, trees with no leaf, no flowers, no city, and no markets. They couldn't see things very clearly.

"This place is hot like desert," said Jennifer.

"I don't feel hot," said Frankie.

"Of course, you are a robot."

"I will protect all of you. This is my purpose of being a robot."

"Thanks."

"It is kind of dark here," said Alan.

"Don't worry!" said Frankie. "I have a flashlight function here." Frankie pressed the button and turned on the flashlight.

"How should we look for Jomo?" said Isabelle.

"Does Frankie have a GPS function?" said Catherine.

"Yes, but the signal is weak here," said Daniel.

"Better than nothing. How long does its battery gonna last? Any backup battery?"

"Yes, I have five backup batteries that last for three days each depending how much Frankie uses its functions."

"I see. OK, let's use the GPS from Frankie now."

"Frankie has no idea how Jomo looks like, so no data. It needs the picture to collect data and search for the person. Do you have a photo of him by any chance?"

"No. Jomo and I rushed to your store without bringing my handbag," said Isabelle.

"Wait, I have a family picture that we took last time Catherine and I were on Earth," said Alan.

"Really?" said Catherine.

"Yes."

Alan took out the picture and gave it to Frankie. Frankie scanned Jomo and searched for his location.

"I found it."

"Where?" asked Isabelle.

"Where is my son?" asked Kimberly.

"Where is he?" asked Daniel.

"He is somewhere in a castle," said Frankie.

"Show us the way. We will follow you," said Isabelle.

"It will take us one hour to get there."

"No problem. Just lead the way."

They walked nonstop through the forest and the mountain. Frankie lost the GPS signal.

"I lost the signal, but it should be around here." Isabelle and the rest were worried. Just when their hope was gone, Isabelle saw Jomo's wedding ring. She picked it up right away.

"This is our wedding ring. Did he drop it here purposely or was he captured by others and dropped the ring here?"

"Either way, at least we know Jomo was once here, so I think he should be somewhere around here," said Catherine.

"I agree."

"Let's continue to search and stay closer together."

"Yup."

They walked different directions to search but he was nowhere to be found. Then all of a sudden, the light grew in the rainbow necklace. The rainbow necklace flew and stopped in the air, then moved again.

"Let's follow the rainbow necklace. Jomo should be near here since his blood is in there. This is our last source to find Jomo," said Daniel.

They followed the rainbow necklace and walked for another two hours until they saw the old castle. They rushed to the castle but couldn't enter the castle as there were many robots as soldiers to protect the queen.

"We only have Frankie and several of us here," said Jennifer.

"Maybe Daniel can figure out a way to stop those robots," said Catherine.

"Me?" said Daniel.

"Yes. You are the one who has created your own robots. You are an expert in this field."

"I am not one hundred percent sure how to control or stop those robots."

"Please try."

"Let's see…hmmm…delete their data, remove their batteries, or use up all their batteries."

"Good ideas, but how are you going to do it? There are so many of them. It's time consuming to take them down one by one."

"Still thinking…"

"We need to find a better approach to deal with them. Can't risk going out like this. Let's wait here and find a way to go in."

They waited until nighttime to find an opportunity to go in. They saw those robots were sitting down. Then another group of robots came out to do the night shift. The first group of robots from the day shift closed their eyes to charge themselves.

"Really? Another group. This is nonstop," said Jennifer.

"I knew the queen won't take the risk to have all robots to go no battery," said Daniel.

"I have a plan," said Catherine.

"What's the plan?"

"Set small fires in different areas. Then, for the ones who are sitting to charge themselves, we have to take off their uniforms and put them on us. This way, after we enter the castle, we can pretend to be them."

Catherine then faced Frankie, "We don't know how many robots there. We will follow you to learn how to be a robot."

"OK," said Frankie.

Daniel, Alan, and Frankie set fire at different locations around the castle. Catherine, Isabelle, and Jennifer walked quietly to the first group of robots and took off some of their uniforms. They then changed their clothes. Soon, Daniel, Alan, and Frankie joined them and got changed, too. They saw the door was opened and ran in quickly before others found out.

Inside the castle, they saw many unique and antique objects with portraits of different queens. They had no idea where to start. The castle was super huge. They entered from room to room.

"Should we go different ways to search for Jomo?" asked Kimberly.

"No, it is hard to find each other later on. We should stay together and work together as a team. Several brains are better than just one brain," said Catherine. They all agreed and nodded their heads.

They continued to search the rooms for hours. When they were tired, they saw the long hallway at the other end of the room; they found an elegant room like a ballroom. They entered the room but no one was there. All of them sat down to rest for a bit except for Frankie. Frankie walked around and accidentally moved the crystal cube in a jade bowl. Suddenly, the room started to shake, and the bookshelf moved to another side. Then, a door opened on its own.

"A secret place?" asked Jennifer.

"It should be. Let's go in," said Isabelle.

They entered the door and saw Jomo locked up in a cage. Isabelle, Daniel, and Kimberly rushed over to the cage.

"Oh my god, I finally found you," cried Isabelle.

"I have missed you. I know you would be able to find me. I dropped the wedding ring as a hint for you to find me," said Jomo.

Frankie used its strength to break the cage. Jomo exited the cage. Jennifer and Isabelle hugged him. Daniel and Kimberly also went to hug him. He was shocked by Daniel and Kimberly's action.

"My son," said Daniel and Kimberly who interrupted their conversation.

"What did you just call me? You two are from the robots' shop," said Jomo.

"We finally found you. You are our son," cried Kimberly.

"Yup, you are our son," cried Daniel.

"I'm confused here. Are you sure you two are my parents?"

"Yes. You have a sakura mark on your back, right?" asked Daniel.

"Yup."

"Could we see your mark?" asked Daniel. Jomo showed them the mark on the back.

"Yes, that's the same mark as our son."

"I was told that my parents are already dead."

"Who told you that?"

"My parents' friend."

"Are you talking about Emily?"

"Yes."

"I don't know why she told you that. When you were little, we got kidnapped to the dimension. Then, your mom and I had serious disease, so we left you to Emily. We don't want you to get our disease. After we recovered, we returned to look for you and Emily, but you guys disappeared."

"Maybe Emily thought we didn't survive from our disease," said Kimberly.

"Maybe. Anyway, I am glad that we found you."

"Let me ask you why did you kidnap Jennifer?"

"Because we needed Catherine and Alan to help us find our son. You vanished from that dimension, and I heard Catherine and Alan protect the dimension. So, we thought if we kidnapped Jennifer, we could get Isabelle to enter the portal and look for her parents. But don't worry, we didn't hurt Jennifer," explained Daniel.

"I see. Mom and Dad, we are finally together."

"We have waited for you to call us for a long time," said Kimberly. They sobbed and embraced each other tightly.

"I know you guys are happy to see each other, but let's leave the talk for later. We need to leave now. We don't know when the queen and other robots will appear," said Catherine.

They rushed to the door but the gate was closed. The queen from the far end clapped hands and appeared in front of them.

"Hi, everyone. Such a touching scene just now. I'm thrilled for you, but that's the end of your happiness. Because I will make you all to be my slaves, then I will make robots that look like you all. After that, you all will go to heaven," said the queen.

"Who are you?" said Daniel.

"She is Queen Jasmine," said Jomo.

"Yup, I am the queen in this dimension. Ha ha ha!"

Queen Jasmine called her robots to come in and ordered them to put them to jail. They had no choice but to follow the robots. After the robots put them in jail, they left and stood outside of the prison.

Catherine whispered, "We could escape here using the rainbow necklace, and one drop of blood from Jomo or Daniel."

"That's a good idea, but we have to return to this dimension because I don't want the queen to control everything here. I need to find a way to make this dimension peaceful," said Alan.

"Agreed. We need to go back to Earth to get help. Jennifer, Daniel, Kimberly, and Frankie need to look for other robots for help. Jomo and Isabelle need to reach out to Kokochu, and then meet up with Jennifer. Alan and I will look for Master Mo and Shu Wei. The more help we get, the stronger we are. We are very weak now. After we gather everyone, we will all rejoin at Isabelle's home," said Catherine.

They all nodded their heads. Then, they used the same way to exit the dark dimension. Queen Jasmine was livid when the robots reported to her that they were no longer there. She ordered robots to look for them otherwise they would be destroyed for being useless.

Soon, they were back to Earth and went different ways to look for help. Isabelle stayed with Jomo. Jomo reached out to Kokochu on his watch, but no answer so he left a message. Daniel and Kimberly took out more powerful weapons and robots. Jennifer was impressed about it. Catherine and Alan went to the secret garden to look for Master Mo and Shu Wei but they weren't there, so they left a note there.

They rejoined at Isabelle's home to wait for a response from Kokochu, Master Mo and Shu Wei. They waited for three days for Kokochu to reply back to Jomo. The message from Kokochu to Jomo stated that he would be there as soon as possible after he takes care of some business on planet Hana.

While waiting, Frankie and the robots taught Jennifer how to use the weapons. She had an in-depth training for a few days. Frankie was the one that trained Jennifer very hard because Frankie wanted her to be safe.

Master Mo and Shu Wei appeared in front of everyone after five days.

"Long time no see," said Master Mo.

"Yup, hello everyone," said Shu Wei.

"We need your support, Shu Wei and Master Mo," said Catherine.

"I know, we saw the note," said Master Mo.

"I am happy you two are here now. We are just waiting for Kokochu to come. He will be here anytime."

As soon as Catherine said that, Kokochu arrived. Jomo and Isabelle went over to hug Kokochu.

"Hi, Kokochu," said Isabelle.

Jomo and Kokochu did a high five with each other. Kokochu waved to others and went over to Jennifer.

"Wow, Jennifer, you are a big girl now. The last time I saw you, you were still two years old."

"Really?"

"Yup."

Jamie came home and was amazed to see everyone. "Mom and Dad, I have missed you two. Welcome home."

"We came back this time to ask for help to save the dark dimension."

"Oh, I see. Hi Isabelle, Jomo, and Jennifer. Who are the other people?"

"This is Daniel, my dad, and Kimberly, my mom. You heard of Shu Wei, Master Mo, and Kokochu. The others are robots, and Frankie is also the robot," said Jomo. Jamie waved and greeted them.

Jamie faced Jomo and said, "I am pleased you found your parents, Jomo."

"Let's leave the talk for later. We have an urgent matter to deal with right now. We are going to the dark dimension, but we will be back," said Catherine.

"OK, I will wait for you all here. Be safe. I need all of you to return here safely," said Jamie.

"Sure," said everyone.

Without delay, they opened the portal and entered the dark dimension together.

Chapter 15

They returned to the castle. They saw the robots and fought with them until they were broken; their data were deleted, and they had run out of batteries. They knocked down all one thousand robots. Then, they ran into the castle and called Queen Jasmine to come out. She came out from the secret gate.

"So brave for coming back after escaping from here. I guess you all want to die today. I changed my mind of turning you all to be my slaves and creating robots of your appearances. Die now," said Queen Jasmine.

Catherine, Alan, Isabelle, Jomo, Daniel, Kimberly, Frankie, Jennifer, Kokochu, Master Mo, Shu Wei, and robots went ahead to fight with Queen Jasmine. Those robots and Frankie used the special weapons of electric swords to shock Queen Jasmine. As for Kokochu, Master Mo, and Shu Wei, they used their powers and magic to attack her. Catherine, Alan, Isabelle, Jennifer, Jomo, Daniel and Kimberly used archery arrows and bows to attack her. Queen Jasmine turned weak and rushed to her treasure box to get the bottle. She drank it, and she returned to normal and became much more powerful than before. She also grabbed the thick robe as her weapon. She sent the power to the robe and stabbed them. They lost the energy, and those robots were almost running out of battery for using it so much. They were mostly injured, weak, and collapsed to the floor.

Queen Jasmine walked to Jennifer. When she was trying to stab Jennifer with her special sword, Frankie went over to cover and protect Jennifer. Frankie fell down and was almost unconscious, feeling weak like a person.

Jennifer cried, "Please don't die. Although you are a robot, I still love you. I want you to be my boyfriend. Get up! Get up! Get up!"

"I also love you but I was afraid to tell you the truth because I am not a human," said Frankie.

"I don't care."

"I am glad to hear that. Bye bye."

Frankie was unconscious.

"Ha ha ha. Don't worry, you are gonna die with the robot," said Queen Jasmine.

"You!" scouted Jennifer. She stood up and took out the rainbow necklace. She went to her father and Daniel for a drop of the blood to go back to Earth. Since they were injured, she put a drop of blood of both Jomo and Daniel. After she obtained the blood on the rainbow necklace, Queen Jasmine ran over quickly to take it.

"How dare you try to escape here again. I won't let that happen," said Queen Jasmine.

All of a sudden, the rainbow necklace was shaking. With the blood of both Daniel and Jomo on the rainbow necklace, the rainbow necklace turned into a powerful weapon. The light from the rainbow necklace shot directly to Queen Jasmine's heart. She collapsed to the floor.

Jennifer went over to check whether or not she was breathing. She was found dead. A yellow rabbit came out of the rainbow necklace.

"Hi, I'm the owner of the rainbow necklace. My name is Rachel. I was in this rainbow necklace for many years."

"Hi Rachel, why are you inside the rainbow necklace? What is your connection with my dad and grandfather? How come they are able to come here with a drop of one of their blood? How come my grandfather has the power to make the store big and small using the rainbow necklace?" asked Jennifer.

"Young lady, so many questions. The rainbow necklace was passed down from one owner to the others. They treated me badly and tossed me away except for one owner who treated me nicely. That person was Leon, Daniel's dad. He was a really good person. He treated the rainbow necklace very kindly, so I appeared in front of him. He was shocked, but we ended up being friends. One time, I was crossing the street and almost hit by the car. Leon came out to protect me. I didn't get injured but Leon was in a bad condition."

"Then what happened afterward?"

"Leon was holding the rainbow necklace with blood in his hand. He told me to take good care of Daniel, and then he was sent to the hospital, but it was too late."

Daniel heard the conversation between Jennifer and Rachel about his father. He walked up to them slowly. He faced Rachel.

"I just know my dad was hit by the car, and he liked the rainbow necklace a lot. Oh, why do we have access to this dark dimension," said Daniel.

"Yup! After Leon's death, I put a spell on the rainbow necklace that only you and Leon's offspring can activate the rainbow necklace to enter the dimension in case of danger from Earth. I also put a spell on you all to transform from humans to creatures whenever you enter the dimension to avoid any issues as an outsider there. Then, whenever you return to Earth, you all are being transformed back to humans. However, I noticed that the spell doesn't work all the time. Sorry! I made a mistake. I think it is safer on Earth than the dimension."

"Then what is this dark dimension about?"

"At the beginning, the dimension was called Bunny Hop Land, but it was destroyed and controlled by Queen Jasmine. She killed all the rabbits and my family. I was powerless at that time. I could only stay inside the rainbow necklace, and it flew to Earth by chance. I couldn't save Leon. I was really weak. After that, I told myself that I needed to be strong in order to protect Daniel and his family. I don't want any tragedy to happen ever again. I had undergone a difficult training with Master Mo."

"I see."

"I can grant you all two wishes as to repay Leon for saving my life."

"I want all our loved ones here to be cured," said Daniel.

"I also wish you could break my grandparents' curse and go back to Earth to live with us," said Jennifer.

"OK, I will grant you these two wishes."

Rachel said magic words in front of the rainbow necklace, and the rainbow necklace grew. Right at that moment, all their loved ones were back to normal like before. Catherine and Alan's pass to the other dimension disappeared.

Master Mo woke up and saw Rachel. He said, "Hi, long time no see. I am proud to have you as my disciple. Thanks for saving us."

"No problem. You are my master forever," beamed Rachel. Master Mo smiled back at her.

Rachel sent everyone back to Earth. She also destroyed the dark dimension. She then vanished with the rainbow necklace.

Catherine, Alan, Isabelle, Jomo, Jamie, Daniel, Kimberly, Jennifer, Frankie, Kokochu, Master Mo and Shu Wei gathered together at Isabelle's home.

"Hi, everyone, welcome back. Good to see you all safe," said Jamie.

She faced Catherine and Alan, "Mom and Dad, glad you are both back. When are you leaving again?" said Jamie.

"This time, we are not going to leave," said Catherine.

"Why? What about the curse?"

"No more curse for us. We have no access to the dimension anymore. We will stay here from now on."

"Really? Are you joking?"

"No, it's for real."

"Yeah!"

They hugged each other. Isabelle also went to hug her parents and Jamie. Catherine and Alan were excited to return home without going to the other dimension. Isabelle and Jamie felt pleased to see their parents back. Jomo, Daniel and Kimberly were happy that they found each other and live together from now on. As for Jennifer and Frankie, they were pleased they were both safe. The others didn't reject their human and robot relationship as long as it's true love. Isabelle and Jomo were also joyful to see Jennifer's happiness and being safe.

Catherine called her brother, Raymond to come for a reunion. He came. That night, they had a warm and enjoyable meal together. After the meal ended, Kokochu returned to planet Hana. Master Mo and Shu Wei also returned to where they belonged. Catherine, Alan, Isabelle, Jomo, Jamie, Jennifer, Frankie, Raymond, Daniel, and Kimberly were finally able to live together under the same roof. They would remember their adventures forever.

CPSIA information can be obtained
at www.ICGtesting.com
Printed in the USA
BVHW030407270822
645604BV00016B/1689